raindrips to Rethfernhim series #2

Canadian Cataloging in Publication Data
Plumley, Rosina
The Japanese Fire Tree
978-1-895166-27-9
1. Fiction. I. Title. II. Series.
Printed and bound in North America
First published 2019
This edition published in 2022
Published by Inconsequential Diversions

*Humph is in his doge. Words weigh no more to him
than raindrips to Rethfernhim.*
– James Joyce, *Finnegan's Wake*

The Japanese Fire Tree

an unbiased account of
the notorious art crime

Rosina Plumley

"One imagines this comfortable son of a bitch thinking of himself as Arthur Rimbaud. As he places that I on the paper he is, in all his mediocrity, more puissant than the shade that he has turned into a 'character'."
– Gilbert Sorrentino, Splendide-Hôtel

Inconsequential Diversions

A Smashing
Dramatic Story
of
American Life

The Japanese Fire Tree includes not only the finest available fictional and actual characters but also government and city officials, church, and club leaders who volunteered their services to appear in several big dramatic scenes. This is:

The Cast of Characters

Blanche Christie – factory worker, singer

Zach Lennox – actor, boyfriend of Blanche

Keith Warner – Blanche's neighbor, voyeur, vet

Stella Campeau – baker, activist

James Ross III – publisher, art connoisseur

Ruby Hillyer – 20,000 pharmaceutical shares

Tennessee Butler – "The King of Steak"

Belle Brooks – angry street artist in black trousers

Donal McGraith – bad attitude, reads French theory

And a host of others

Big in Drama, Big in Names, Big in its Pull on the Emotions

hope is the leash of submission

PART 1

1.

It was August, 2018. Let's just call it 1984.

At this time of night the narrow street below always had an after-the-party look of exhaustion. Marked by absence, disrespected with discarded debris. From his third floor perch Keith glimpsed the furtive movements of a cat emerging from gloom then immediately sliding, liquid, back into shadow as if embarrassed by being the last guest to leave.

Keith's eyes moved to take in the abandoned, boarded up factory across the street. The one slightly to his right.

A shifting light had just appeared in the narrow bank of windows near the top of the building. A slow irregular pulse of varying colors. This was the fourth time in three weeks he'd observed these lights in the early morning hours.

With sudden resolve and wine-manufactured courage, Keith donned his running shoes, went downstairs, and crossed the narrow road.

He shinnied up a parking sign growing out of the sidewalk and with a well-timed move launched himself sideways to grab the bottom rung of the fire escape bolted to the wall, and pulled himself up.

He climbed. At the top, he pushed his face up to one of the chicken wire ribbed panes of glass, and leaning slightly forward, looked down.

The view inside was limited, both because of the angle and the lack of illumination, but immediately below him the end of a mattress was visible. A small television with an antenna was perched atop it. The TV was on – the obvious source of the dancing lights. And there was what looked to be a clock sitting beside the TV, also on the mattress. Abutting it, the head of another old striped mattress was visible. Newspapers and litter were strewn across that one.

A hand came into view, slightly adjusted the position of the TV antenna, and then withdrew.

Keith continued to stare, but there were no further glimpses of the person.

From the sidewalk beneath him came the sound of voices. He crouched down out of the light. Invisible beneath the windows, he watched while the slow wave of noise from a couple, squeezing together as if attached, passed by.

The pair were animated, their words colliding, making love in an unashamed orgy of sound that interrupted the night.

"And I did," the male voice said.

"And not her?" the woman asked over top of him.

"No, no."

"I thought it was her."

"No, not, how could it be?"

The night settled back into calm as the voices receded.

Keith retreated to the sidewalk and then home.

Later, laying in his bed, Keith wondered about the factory squatter, who she was and how she'd come to be living in such conditions. What misfortunes had befallen her?

Keith had already assigned the person a gender and even sculpted an image of her. He began to formulate the idea of a rescue, and, since he was an aspiring photo journalist, he thought that this might also be the subject of an article. He could follow the woman, photograph her, make out the story of her life and downfall. Was it for economic reasons? Drugs? Was she a criminal in hiding? Perhaps he'd have to crop the photos for his article to hide her identity.

Keith didn't consider the possibility that he might be a stalker. His motives were pure, after all. Benevolent. The piece could raise awareness of her plight, and that of other homeless people. Surely no one would choose such a life.

When it came to women, and life in general, Keith was heavily engaged in fantasy and dreams because of his isolation, to the point where they often obliterated reality.

Eventually, he'd had enough for one day and went to bed.

Keith's interest in photo journalism, as a means of rescue, stemmed from his belief in the transformative power of looking. But – not unlike many men with such noble intentions – the subject of his fantasy heroics were invariably beautiful Eliza Doolittles. A very select sort of charity.

On Keith's bedroom wall was a print of Pre-Raphaelite painter Edward Burne-Jones's *King Cophetua and the Beggar Maid,* a depiction of a king brought down through the act of looking, by the sight of the beggar maid as he looked down at the street through a window.

Everyone in the painting looked at the erotically clad maid from a distance. Some looked down at her but the King was at her feet looking up. At her idealized beauty.

The woman on a pedestal is viewed from this perspective, obviously, which also indicates a lack of perceived humanity; the inability to conceive of her reality or return her gaze, the perception of her in ideal terms, as if she were a statue.

The Pygmalion story – which Eliza Doolittle was based on – told of a sculptor who crafted a statue of the perfect woman because she did not exist in nature. But this Platonic ideal became reality when the sculpture came to life. Perhaps the essence of male fantasy; that our solopsistic world with its fantasies can be given reality. Pygmalion was a primary subject of Burne-Jones.

2.

Stella was asleep.

Shifts of her torso and hands told that she was dreaming.

She had once hugged Kalie, at the bar, but Kalie quickly pushed back saying that Stella was crushing her.

Stella thought about it afterwards. Kalie's response hadn't been the fragility and brittleness of a princess afraid of the crudeness of another body, like those "soft cherubic creatures" ridiculed by Emily Dickinson. Kalie was just tiny.

Unacknowledged by Stella was that she may have held on too tightly because overcoming all of her loneliness had been contained in that joyful squeeze. It was bound to have been overwhelming.

In her dream, she rested her cheek against Kalie's.

Stella's thoughts played over Kalie's face in minute detail, re-constructing it, sculpting a likeness, appreciating the features fine and delicate, almost like a child's.

She touched Kalie's face with her fingertips.

Kalie didn't withdraw and Stella smiled in her sleep.

Born in 1880, Helen Keller, was both deaf and blind. The tragic outcome of a childhood illness

Yet she became not only an accomplished woman but a political one as a pacifist, member of the Wobblies, co-founder of the American Civil Liberties Union, socialist, activist, advocate for birth control and suffrage, and author. She would write that blindness was a social and political outcome.

Her means of breaking out of her isolation, of her understanding and desire to transform the world, was accomplished through experience, reading, intellect and touch. She saw and listened through her fingertips; through direct physical contact. She pronounced Mark Twain a "king" after she touched him, and he later declared her and Napoleon to be the two most interesting people of the 19th Century (a comment devoid of either ego or humorous intention).

Helen Keller lives somewhere near Keith and me.

Perhaps in a condo but maybe in a factory squat.

"Of course there are manifold means used to manufacture the ignorance needed to vote for a fake political party that serves only the wealthy, such as: under funding schools, working to destroy public education through privatization, making post-secondary education prohibitively expensive, devaluing intellectualism, and attacking the idea of objective scientific fact. But one of the simplest continues to be indoctrination through media and public schooling. For example, a news item from September 16, 2018, tells us that in order to 'streamline' their curriculum, a Texas Board of Education has dropped Hillary Clinton and Helen Keller from their curriculum. It's pure Orwell. Down the memory hole. Control the past to control the present."
– Johnny Fellen, blog entry

"This is the Age of Loneliness … The war of every man against every man – competition and individualism, in other words – is the religion of our time, justified by a mythology of lone rangers, sole traders, self-starters, self-made men and women, going it alone. For the most social of creatures, who cannot prosper without love, there is no such thing as society, only heroic individualism. What counts is to win. The rest is collateral damage."
– George Monbiot, 'The age of loneliness is killing us'

3.

The job interview was later that same day, about 3:20 p.m..

Blanche Christie was telling herself to view the interview as an acting audition. A displacement technique for stress, no doubt. She, and a very young looking HR Manager, had by this time spent twenty-five minutes sitting in the factory's mezzanine meeting room waiting on Janine Seaman, the warehouse manager. Between their trite exchanges, Blanche read and reread the inspirational posters on the wall; homilies to teamwork and safety. Niceties, that in her experience always gave way as priorities to maximizing productivity.

The door opened and Seaman strode in wearing jeans and

an orange safety vest. She pronounced, "Let's get going!"

No apology. She was the star among the little people. "Alright Mr. DeMille, I'm ready for my close-up."

Blanche was about to be upstaged. There were only so many starring roles in this hierarchical production – the warehouse management role having always been primarily about supervising a low-wage workforce of mostly women – and hanging on to one of the better jobs meant disinheriting the meek.

Blanche took note of Seaman's unnecessary fluorescent vest and recognized it as a bit of costuming to announce to herself, and the HR manager no doubt, that Seaman was a roll-up-her-sleeves type, and a get-down-on-the-shopfloor-with-the-proles type. An all round "woman of action".

And Blanche knew instinctively that she was trapped in a bad production with a scenery chewing diva. It was not going to be her starring moment.

Utilizing the company's version of Bentham's panopticon, the manager turned to position her chair so that she could look down at the factory floor; an act that demands a metaphorical shift. All her senses were on alert. Below, the women picked and packed orders with dreary, soul-destroying precision. Despite their separation, to avoid such egregious lapses of discipline, snatches of conversation and laughs hung in the air momentarily before dissipating, and each caused Seaman to freeze like a fearful deer caught in the headlights, suddenly aware of the threat from humanity.

And then came the self-serving questions:

"Can you cope in a culture of excellence?"

"My leadership is resulting in tremendous efficiencies. Do you have a high learning curve?"

Seaman didn't take a single note to record Blanche's answers. And she frowned often.

Blanche soon realized that working for Seaman would be a special sort of hell so not getting this particular job would be a blessing in some ways. Her anxiety, which was pretty constant these days, began to subside. She knew the Seaman type: do some useless minor tinkering, schmooze and convince the boss you've made a huge difference, play on their ignorance, back stab and undermine everyone else.

She was already working in a miserable workplace with layers of management, each intent on measuring and gathering data on your every move, visual surveillance having given way to computer surveillance. Every MBA saw making changes to improve on current figures as their path to advancement and riches, although any "improvements" were generally just the result of an increase in bullying.

And then there were the industrial engineers with their reports that they didn't understand, who viewed humans as machines, believing that a person could perform the same minuscule part of a larger process, at rapid speed, without pauses, while maintaining enough concentration to not make mistakes, for eight straight hours.

Lately, after viewing computer records, you were even called on to account for yourself if you took an "unreasonably long" bathroom break. Or, potentially, any sort of bathroom break. Anxiety from something like stage fright, at the internalized sense of being watched, was one way in which stress was cynically ratcheted up as a management tool. What got to you wasn't just a fear of job loss and becoming destitute. Biting your tongue and grovelling meant the undermining of your self esteem and dignity; an essential tool for any authoritarian system.

And, as an additional, "Thank you for your dedicated service", the Ross family who owned the business had outsourced the operation to a third party who were continuing the same practices while paying workers only half as much for their expanded efforts. This was the primary cause of Blanche's dire financial straits.

But there was another reason she'd been particularly hopeful about this interview. It was because she wanted an out from helping her boyfriend Zach in his "theft" of a painting. It wasn't a real theft, the way it had been explained to her, but the idea of it still bothered her.

"You cannot easily fit women into a structure that is already coded as male; you have to change the structure."
– Mary Beard, Women & Power: A Manifesto

"Not merely the validity of experience, but the very existence of external reality, was tacitly denied by their philosophy ... If both the past and the external world exist only in the mind, and if the mind itself is controllable – what then? ... The Party told you to reject the evidence of your eyes and ears. It was their final, most essential command."
– George Orwell, 1984

Blanche's bus ride home was a slow one. The road was clogged with late afternoon traffic belting out toxins and pollutants. Not to worry Blanche, global warming is "fake news" according to The Tribune, the local Ross newspaper, which had lately adopted Trumpian tactics like opposite attribution ("it's the Democrats who lock up kids"), inversion (trumpet every failure as a success, like Puerto Rico relief) and the dissolution of reality (there is no climate change).

Blanche suddenly felt a surge of anger about the unsuccessful job interview she'd just left, recalling the manager's lack of notes, dismissiveness, and refusal to make eye contact. Blanche felt used; a supporting player in a self-promotional drama by the factory manager, staged for the HR manager. She'd been treated as if she was a nothing and invisible. As if she didn't exist. Blanche wished she'd screamed at the manager: LOOK AT ME!

That was a constant in her life. Managers who stole her ideas. Parents who pushed her to live the life they plotted for her. An agent who always felt she knew what was best, trying to make her into a replica of some pop singer or actress whether Blanche wanted it or not. And a boyfriend who dismissed her concerns as if they were delusions.

Both men and women plowed right over her because those with power or money steal the voice of the powerless and render them invisible. In the end, the one with a voice is the one who determines what is real, fake, and important. They control history and shape myth. It happens with the corporately owned newspaper, the art gallery, the politician, the colonizer, the publisher, the record label, and the boss. It happens in any social relationship where there is structural inequality.

Without a book or magazine, and a desolate industrial landscape outside that had obliterated wild nature, replaced, as Jacques Ellul once wrote, by billboards, signs, and images substituting themselves for the reality of nature, Blanche's eyes flitted from one to another of the ubiquitous ads posted around the bus.

A poster advertising a Hawaiian vacation caught her eye. She and her co-worker Billie would often daydream about such a trip and talk about it on their way home.

Blanche longed for escape, if only she could afford it.

The billboard said, "Live a Little", but she misread it as, "Love a Little".

Zach, always the critic, liked to tell her that a Hawaiian vacation is just another product promising happiness that, in the end, doesn't deliver and leaves you feeling deflated and lied to. And on top of that, the fantasy traded on old colonial notions of half-naked Pacific natives living with abandon.

She suspected that the cliché ad imagery itself, of scantily clad women by the sea, sirens, meant mostly for male titillation, was also unsettling to Zach since they shaped his view of the reality of such trips as being about licentious behaviour away from knowing eyes. Sexuality unleashed, real and imagined. She wasn't going to explain to him what was real and not about her motives. Leave him to his own reality.

No one was going to steal her fantasies.

4.

The Zach in question departed his bus, one in a queue discharging pilgrims at the suburban mall. He traveled inside amid the supplicants but, through habit, imagined that all eyes were on him, so he walked with studied nonchalance.

Still, he believed he'd remain anonymous; the current norm. No one would remember him if he defied orders and slid in for a coffee. Not a chance. Besides, he'd be quick as the proverbial bunny since he detested food courts after working some shows in a mall. The steamed, dried out food.

The pimps and other scum who preyed on runaways. The unbearable sadness of the elderly regulars whose desire to be a part of society had been reduced to sitting on the edges of a crowd of people and watching life shuffle by.

But things seldom worked out for Zach any more. Walking away from the coffee bar, a devout sojourner with a young boy in tow approached.

"Can you give me an autograph?" she asked. "I loved *Conor and Biddy*." The reference being to his short-lived cable series of several years back.

"Of course."

The woman rooted in her bag. A Sharpie was handed over. The top buttons of her floral summer dress were opened. Mounds of very pale skin protruded from the top of her bra. She pointed to one side. "Right here," she said.

Zach signed with a practiced, de-sexualized ease, which he didn't feel. The publicist's dream smile as a disguise.

Minutes later, as Zach hastened through the mall, a woman with pink-tipped hair and cocksure attitude fell into step beside him. What were the chances? They began to chat without much ado, about nothing and about no thing. As they neared a card shop the woman said, "That's where I work. I'll be finished at nine." It was said with ambiguity and self-assurance. She didn't pause for an answer.

Zach walked on.

Only for a brief moment did he wonder about the woman. Had she mistaken him for his character? Did she think he could help with her career? Was she attracted to power or celebrity? He didn't much care. The one thing he was certain about was that her interest wasn't in him per se. He had long ago come to that crushing realization. It had been a mostly shattering experience once his fifteen minutes of fame were up, and he wasn't wanted to sell someone's product or show, that a celebrity was a commodity easily disposed of.

For years, because of his celebrity, Zach had hidden his background and built a false identity, becoming the fake Irishman Conor. He'd pimped himself out, selling that identity. In his case by flogging cheap commodities in green packaging with Irish sounding names. He'd have gone full Kardashian but the commercial opportunities for cable stars were limited.

Now though, without the demand to maintain a public

identity, Zach felt free to be a nomad, "with no connection to this culture and place", as he would say. As if nomads have no community! His fondest wish was to buy a camper and live in the south, to escape this city with its frustrations and shameful memories that went for him with their claws in the night. They stopped him from any re-imagining of himself.

You needed to be washed clean of memories by the river Lethe before you could begin again. Virgil wrote that, he'd been told.

Memory was a damnable thing.

Now, he was just an unemployed and broke actor with fantasies of escape. And his music gigs – few and far between – no longer even paid him guaranteed money.

Sometimes Zach lied to his girlfriend Blanche about having a gig in order to restore a bit of his personal dignity, then drove out of town and slept in his car to give the appearance of having played somewhere.

Zach walked across the mall parking lot to its furthest reaches and easily found the copper-colored Eclipse parked there for him, got in and slid on the driving gloves left inside the glove compartment along with the keys.

He drove off. He was going to steal *The Japanese Fire Tree*, a painting he'd been led to believe was worthless.

The $1000 he'd be paid for the robbery wouldn't solve anything – it would only provide a temporary respite, a couple of month's rent on his bachelor apartment – but it was a necessary sacrifice for survival to the gods of consumption.

Life *is* *just* One Success After Another

"Sure, an actor can do some PR and even become a celebrity – yet they can still act. But the pure celebrity has no other skill apart from (often) being the child of a wealthy person. They go by names like Hilton, Jenner, Kardashian, and Trump. They get 'reality shows', have followers, get elected, endorse and sell products. The intense desire for attention is always infantile. They are self-marketers, selling the idea not only that they have skills but that they live in a higher reality of glamour, empowerment, and riches.

And some people want to believe that this chimera is real life, more real than their own crappy life and something to aspire to. As Raoul Vaneigem wrote: 'Hope is the leash of submission.'"

– Phil O'Lodge. The Kirkland Lake Memoirs

5.

At 6:30 p.m., as usual, James Ross III strode between the cubicles in The Tribune's newsroom. He sanctified with a nod and smile, sans actual eye contact, those supplicants sitting behind their desks who looked up as he passed.

"Nice job on the new church piece, Janice," James said, looking off into the distance as he spoke, basking in his voice's deep timbre and the moral purity of the remark, which hung in the air after him. He left the building and climbed into his late model Mercedes convertible.

Work on the following morning's edition was all but wrapped up and he felt the satisfaction of knowing that it looked great.

James took his responsibilities as publisher seriously.

Lead news story would be a feel good piece about a returning soldier meeting his newborn son for the first time. Human interest stories sold papers. The piece was followed by a whole page of photos, including a shot of the Stars and Stripes and another of a soldier saluting the President. Inexpensive, heart-tugging filler. The other front page stories involved a lemonade stand and a woman who was walking across the country to express her love for America.

There were two conservative think tank editorials on the usual subjects: the "need" for less taxes for "job creators" and the threat of the "foreign funded" climate change hoax.

Ross Media owned The Tribune, and Ross Media was owned by James III. He was a member of, and heir to, the Ross family businesses. His family was the richest in the state and the major employer, so they were bowed to and lavishly praised by politicians, although the wage levels in this needy state were among the lowest in the country.

The Ross media syndicate was often subject to ridicule by liberal residents because the newspaper, not unexpectedly, promoted family interests and provided only the most minimal information – if any – on the multiple lawsuits and criticisms of Ross businesses. Protesters at Ross Lumber operations frequently carried banners quoting from Orwell's *1984:* IGNORANCE IS STRENGTH.

III opened the top of the convertible before adjusting his shades and setting off. This was a wonderful day, yet one that he was certain would only get better.

"'Fake news,' 'post truth,' 'alternate facts', and 'truth' that can change in mid sentence, are all signs of an existential crisis for people who will discount their inner experience of reality to align it with what an authority figure pronounces to be actual reality, even in the face of its obvious untruth. It overcomes a sense of impotence, as does supporting attacks and insults against others put forth without evidence. The latter confirms that satisfaction is derived from the venting, from the name calling experience itself and not the truth of the insult, as even children know.

These are primary reasons why many people opted for a know-nothing, loud-mouthed fool as their political leader. Not that Trump is Hitler, but as Adorno once wrote of Hitler, his being a clown wasn't beside the point, it was the point. It's not that there is now a group knowingly directing some ontological hocus pocus. It's just the same old gang using the same old tools of propaganda, snake oil and lies for their own gain, and mostly doing it with ineptitude and failure, their schemes forever blowing up in their faces."

– Joe Palumbo, Introduction to More Symbolic Plumbing

"Although very different from what Antonin Artaud intended with his Theater of Cruelty – to overcome the violence in our lives – what is happening with Donald Trump has the quality of an Artaud spectacle. It is an attack on intellectual truth, creating fear and chaos, conducted with incoherent gibberish, madness, sex, and violence in order to connect directly with the audience and their senses.

Its ultimate aim is the destruction of rational discourse. Watch the rally audiences – even the unpaid members – as they take on roles, participating in the spectacle, becoming actors, chanting on cue from the director. They let the holy spirit invade them. Objective facts no longer exist."
– Nikita Sunburn, Camp Sunburn

6.

It was close to 7:00 p.m. when Blanche steered Zach's Grand Am on to the packed expressway – an open wound through unceded First Nations' land – leading to the suburbs and out of town. She slowed the car by necessity.

Without a better paying job there was now no getting out of participating in Zach's robbery. Her first response to his appeal for her help with the scheme had been moral repugnance and a flat out refusal, but it was explained to her, repeatedly, that it was only a "fake robbery".

Zach had a friend named Davey, an overly friendly sort who reeked of insincerity and invited all the un-Edenish temptations arising when meeting a big snake when you have a garden shovel in hand. Davey, on behalf of the restauranteur Tennessee Butler, had approached Zach with the plan.

Butler wanted someone to break into his own house – currently occupied by his estranged wife – and "steal" an old oil painting that he owned. The art had only sentimental value and was being held hostage by a vindictive woman who Butler was in the process of divorcing. He was fed up, according to Davey, sick of paying lawyers and of his wife's refusal to give him the art despite a court order. It was time to act. A fake robbery would get the painting back and allow Butler to disavow having taken any part in the act.

Blanche had other reservations about the plan. Butler, it was said, was engaged in criminal activity and his restaurant was apparently frequented by the holy trinity of the greedy: mob bosses, Ross owned politicians, and businessmen in $3000 suits with paid escorts attached to their silken sleeves. He definitely wasn't someone she wanted any involvement with and argued that Zach shouldn't have any either. It was a risky endeavor, in spite of Davey's assurances. A robbery was still a robbery. And there was no guarantee that Butler would even pay them once the painting was retrieved.

But when she made her arguments to Zach he steamrolled over them, barely listening, smiling at what he presumably took to be feminine timidity, while responding with tut tutting, and not to worry your little head over it paternalism. She always loathed the idea that Zach might see her as some bird-brained groupie like those who besieged him at times, and that this was the source of his dismissiveness.

In the end, she agreed to help with the robbery, not from Zach's persuasiveness as he no doubt felt, but out of sympathy for him, knowing that he was pushing the idea so much because he was flat broke.

There was no doubt too, that the $2000 they would split after the robbery would enable her to make her condo payments for a couple of months. And that was imperative. She couldn't bear the thought of losing the place. She'd scraped and saved for a down payment over two years and buying the condo had positively changed her life. Once again she felt independent and integrated into society. And in control. These were keys to her recovery.

For once, she hoped that the vultures who would swoop in on Zach when he was in public, with items to autograph, including themselves, and proffering phone numbers, had cornered Zach on some street. She was sure that he'd bask in the attention, and hopefully enough to forget the robbery.

"The old photograph I am looking at is far more appealing than any air-brushed ideal. There is something beautiful in old photos with their imperfections and disintegration. As objects, as life, they defy the contention that art is immortal by reflecting natural, melancholic transformation, as surely as the trees in autumn that Schiele painted.

And what also emerges is something unexpected and stunning. My gaze drifts over this woman's face and lingers on the imperfections of her skin, her fatigue, her eyes looking back. My gaze is an act of intimacy that quickly fades to melancholy. To look at this face feels like a violation. With no relationship between myself and the woman, my gaze is voyeuristic. Could it be otherwise given the separations of life and the privilege of the viewer of art? And my sense of shame is quickly strengthened because of the sudden revelation that this woman is beautiful. Not the contemporary air-brushed and uniform sort of beauty, perfect and non-existent, but as artists and lovers know, the wondrous beauty of nature in every human, striking when we stop and note it. We don't see something that isn't there, but discover what is there but has remained unremarked.

Do I imagine it or are this peasant woman's eyes searching for a reciprocal response? They make me think of a past, prior to enclosure and the destruction of peasant communities and autonomy, when looking was a mutual interaction between connected people — eyes looking into eyes — before photographic, mediating, commodified imagery became instances of uninvited intimacy. To see this beauty causes us to long to overcome our isolation at the same time as providing consolation for our loss of the connections to nature and to others."
— Craig Grimes, On Writing

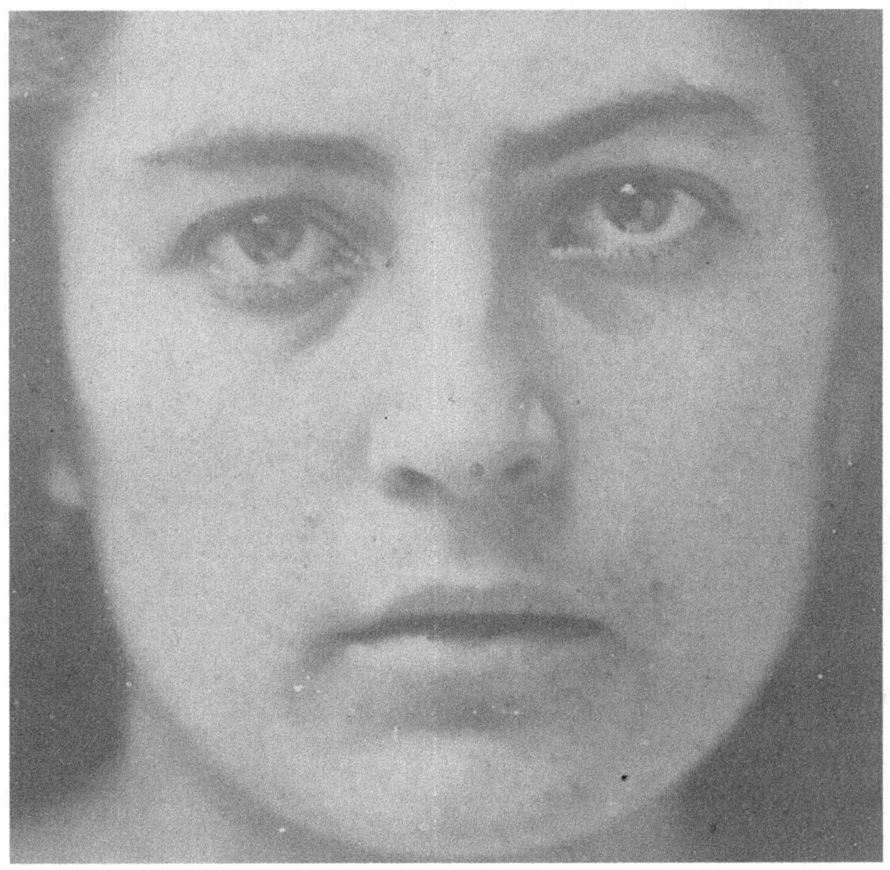

"Traditionally the gaze was conceived of as a way of fingering. The old Greeks spoke about looking as a way of sending out my psychopodia[?], my soul's limbs to touch your face and establish a relationship between the two of us which is this relationship, and this relationship was called vision."
– Ivan Illich, interview with Jerry Brown

"I saw in one hour that both nature and woman were alive with indescribable radiance – with beauty. This was a revelation ... I think the consciousness of beauty is awakened in individuals as in peoples by a prolonged unsatisfied desire. Perhaps the modern feeling for the beauty of nature as a peculiar quality – an expression of divine ecstasy rather than a mere decoration of the world – arose when men began to look on everything about them with the unsatisfied longing which has its proper analogue in puberty."
– J.M. Synge, Autobiography

7.

Charles Ross, for all his crassness, was an accomplished man of business who intuitively understood the unstated first principle of the art market: if a thing has no monetary value then it has no aesthetic value.

The Japanese Fire Tree was one of a number of Egon Schiele's stark landscape paintings, of angular trees, done mostly between 1911 and 1913. The near bankrupt businessman who sold the work to Charles, in 1953, told him that he'd purchased it in Vienna in 1919. Charles recalled the year well. It was the year his son, grandiosely known as James The First, was born. It was also the year that Charles began his newspaper, The Tribune. And it was the same year he'd paid to have a union organizer fomenting trouble among the workers in his logging camps dealt with. The unfortunate man was shot in the face by one of Charles' policemen while making a union speech. None of the man's claims alleging the camps were unsafe, filthy, and rampant with dysentery, were reported in The Tribune. Nor was the man's death.

Charles didn't like the painting. The subject was "spindly", "foreign", and "ugly". Plus, the piece made him uncomfortable. It depicted a small maple, with twisted limbs dancing in a contorting wind, the naked branches forming a geometric pattern. Charles would say how he preferred "a mighty oak" or "a majestic pine", trees that could even inspire one to poetry. Those trees were money. Maples were "garbage trees" that no one bought.

It was Charles' wife Teresa who wanted the painting. She was from blue blood European aristocracy although she wasn't personally affected by the generations of family inbreeding whose problems would emerge as an issue for her descendants.

Teresa was sharp enough to understand public perception and public image. To purchase art was to purchase refinement. And in this case, it might even whitewash the public image of a cutthroat capitalist like her Charles who fleeced governments for money and owned all the important politicians.

The Japanese Fire Tree was being sold for a song but by the time Charles got through with the desperate seller, the guy was almost ready to pay him to take the thing off his hands. He even tossed in several lesser paintings to seal the deal.

When Charles asked Teresa, "What's so good about Schiele?" she replied that, "He has an eye."

This made no sense to Charles. Now he had an eye, he told himself. He'd started small, in lumber, and over the years expanded laterally into pulp and paper, and lumber stores. Later, he was convinced about the future of the automobile and had bought into oil and gas manufacture with an idea to expand into service stations and home heating sales.

Charles had an eye for business.

After Teresa's death, Charles had the troublesome, ugly painting, along with his wife's other "art", moved to the attic.

"By definition art is fakery, a lie. In this, Plato is correct. The word 'original' when attached to an art object functions solely as an advertising slogan. An original cannot have more aesthetic value than an exact copy. If the copy is exact then there is no difference in the experience. The original is entirely about money. It is a relic ... We are paying homage to an absence. If there is any truth to the aesthetic theory, that some good lies in the object made, then the authenticity is irrelevant. Whether it is a Picasso or not is irrelevant. If the pedigree is paramount than the aesthetic is minor, perhaps irrelevant, and what we have is a relic. ... The insistence on authenticity and provenance in art only serves the wealthy. These characteristics are meant to determine a monetary value not an aesthetic one. The assertion that art has been made by [a certain famous] artist has no aesthetic value nor can it."
– Donal McGraith, Leaving No Mark

8.

Standing in the hallway of his mansion, James Ross III glanced at his Rolex for the fifth time in fifteen minutes and yelled at Ruby to hurry up.

"Shake your tail, babe!"

Normally he didn't mind Ruby doddling, she could make quite an eyeful, but tonight they had a schedule to keep to.

James looked at his Rolex with something like fondness and pulled it down on his wrist so that it would remain visible. He liked to show off his stuff, and that – to his way of thinking – included Ruby. Enviable eye candy, and from a very wealthy family to boot! She was twenty-three, a businesswoman and a member of Friends of the Gallery. James liked that she had the look of a fashion model. (I doubt I'm the only one who cringes when I see wealthy men, like James Ross III, with much younger trophy partners on their arms.) The source of all James's value judgments and aspirations was based on surface and appearance insofar as they reflected wealth. Looking was everything; truth itself.

James was forty-four years old. His hair was patchy and his stomach was actively exploring new dimensions of space, but he knew he looked good and that he was envied. In spite of the fact that he never read anything and got his opinions at the golf course – so he was mostly described by others as a "simpleton" – he never questioned the idea that he was better than others because of his inherited wealth. It went without saying. But the degree to which he assiduously maintained his conspicuous consumption suggested that it was essential to him that he convince others of his view. Perhaps it was a means of self-delusion, to intentionally create his dream reality and escape the self-contempt that might follow from questioning whether he had accomplished anything of significance in his life except to acquire a large pile of useless crap. Or to acknowledge that he was a predictable bore.

(I do recognize though that there are many who would scoff at the idea of James Ross the Third having any degree of self-awareness.)

James knew little about running a business. He eventually grasped that it was comparable to knitting or making a stew. It was functional, skill based knowledge. But it was also like sports. James had learned from James II, Pater Familias, that the secret to success was cheating. Rules were for other people. Business ethics were for suckers.

James III and Ruby had both been engaged to be married to different heirs in the past but at some point had cast their covetous eyes on each other.

They'd first met at a gallery function, and strolled through the modern art wing afterwards. They expressed their business interest in the money to be made from the contemptuous works of the Young British Artists. On this and other matters they seemed to be of one mind. A few weeks later the pair announced their engagement.

Soon after, James joined the gallery's Board of Directors and in no time became Vice-Chair.

James had known nothing of art until three years before meeting Ruby. He'd always been a partier and it had taken a nice donation and a stern lecture from Daddy to get him through two years of university. But on III's thirtieth-fifth birthday his father had given him the family's media holdings and Great-grandfather's "worthless" art, including *The Japanese Fire Tree* by the Austrian artist Egon Schiele.

One day after claiming that portion of his inheritance, James pulled out the paintings, made a list of the artists who'd created them, and looked them up online. Nothing of note. Not until he plunked in the name of Egon Schiele. It was a New York Times headline that read, "Multi-million Dollar Auction Record" that caught his attention.

After that, James set out to learn everything he could about the art business and about Schiele in particular. He scanned online articles, bought books, and made phone calls. One collector in Canada was especially receptive to his attentions. James was crooked, dim-witted, and easily fooled, so an art dealer's dream.

Shortly thereafter, James made his first move in the art world when he donated all of Great-grandfather's paintings – the Schiele excepted – to the local gallery. James was on his way to becoming an art patron and member of a select circle.

He worked closely with his accountant who knew all the tax breaks and loopholes. Art came in and art went out. His collection always expanding and funding itself with clever dealing, speculation, and schemes.

James' mansion had even recently been renovated to properly display his impressive holdings. The interior of the house had been stripped down. Sight lines altered so that art was visible from every room. In one case, an interior wall had been removed to accommodate a huge oil painting. The whole was colored in primary shades of ostentation and draped with textiles of supercilious contempt and snobbery.

A half hour after leaving the mansion, James III and Ruby Sterling made their way between the tables at Tennessee Butler's Steakhouse, nodding and saying hello to the influential patrons they passed, while often stopping to shake hands. Judging by how slowly he moved tonight, James wanted to be seen. And Tennessee Butler's was the place to see and be seen.

On this particular evening the other diners included a state senator, a billionaire, the CEO of a Fortune 500 company, the Federal Secretary of the Treasury, the editor of a nationally renowned newspaper, the mayor, and one of the deans at the local university. And those were just the people who James the Third recognized.

Once James and Ruby were seated, a glowing Tennessee Butler, owner and namesake of the restaurant, arrived at their table to say "Welcome" and to thank James for the positive review that had recently run in the Ross newspapers. The reviewers – "The Two Food Ladies" as they billed themselves – were the world's dullest writers and knew nothing of food, but they did know how to drop superlatives for an establishment owned by a friend of the owner. Besides the meat, they had raved about the starched white linens and "ultra-soft rolls" at Tennessee's. Important stuff no doubt.

James looked at Tennessee and held his eye. "Don't mention it Tennessee," he said. "You got the best steaks in town, just like The Two Food Ladies said."

"Meeting someone's gaze almost immediately engages a raft of brain processes, as we make sense of the fact that we are dealing with the mind of another person who is currently looking at us. In consequence, we become more conscious of that other person's agency, that they have a mind and perspective of their own – and, in turn, this makes us more self-conscious."
– Christian Jarrett, 'Why meeting another's gaze is so powerful'

9.

Zach had saved money during his stint on *Conor and Biddy*, enough to have lasted for years, but instead, he invested it in a weekly entertainment tabloid called "What's On" that covered entertainment events in the state. Initially, it provided listings of music, theater, and films but over time it expanded to include reviews and columns. The paper began to feel more like a calling than a business.

But then the Ross newspaper, The Tribune, happened. They began a competing entertainment weekly and went for "What's On's" advertisers, giving them cut rate terms that Zach couldn't compete with. How does one compete with free? The Tribune went so far as to intimate to several advertisers that since the Ross family wielded such influence with local and state governments, that a refusal to advertise exclusively with their weekly could mean saying goodbye to any government business or grants. Zach had come to feel that the Ross family's crushing of his tiny paper was likely more than just the monopolist's obsessive approach to any competition – no matter how small to acquire and close it. It was also about power; a consolidation of their monopoly to use media to shape public opinion.

In the end, out of money, Zach sold "What's On" to The Tribune for a few dollars and a verbal promise that the weekly would be allowed to continue to operate independently. Immediately, the Sex and the Gay themed columns were gone and a few months later so were both weekly papers. Entertainment listings and reviews were thereafter included in the Thursday edition of The Tribune, available for the cost of a newspaper or online subscription.

10.

Wearing a mask – as he often did, in one form or another – Zach rounded the impressive teardrop driveway and stopped the stolen Eclipse at the foot of the grand staircase fronting the Tennessee Butler mansion, still home to his wife.

Five yards wide at the base, the sweeping stairs narrowed to two yards, eighteen steps up, where they ended between marble columns at the center of the front portico.

"Sweet Jesus," he whispered under his breath. There was obviously a lot of money in steak. The stark, brobdingnagian staircase wouldn't have been out of place in a Leni

Riefenstahl propaganda film glorifying the Nazi empire.

If Zach had known that the house actually belonged to James Ross the Third he would have seen it as a thumbing of his nose towards the peasantry, and a self-aggrandizing statement of superiority from a man he regarded as an entitled and parasitical son-of-a-bitch.

The Eclipse was positioned to its best advantage for the CCTV cameras.

Zach flipped a bird at the camera, a sudden improvisation. Tennessee Butler, author of this play, had been right to accept Davey's recommendation to hire an actor, Zach thought.

Today he was an action hero. Steve McQueen in *The Thomas Crown Affair*. To Tennessee Butler, he was the beaked thug playing third henchman.

"Easy peasy," said Davey after outlining the strategy. "I'll draw you the layout of the house and give you a photo of the painting. A plate attached to the frame says 'The Japanese Fire Tree'."

Zach removed a sledge hammer from the trunk of the car, left the lid up, bounded up the stairs three at a time, and without a pause charged the front door with the hammer held high. He brought it down with might and main. Nothing.

The burglar alarm screamed accusingly, which startled him, and he immediately looked to the side and behind. The peaceable world went on. They were out in the country on an estate lot with no visible neighbours and surrounded by forest and fields. Van Gogh, leaning over his easel pitched in a field, was noticeable by his absence. "If a burglar alarm blasts in the forest does anyone hear it?"

It took two more impressive, Herculean, screen-worthy, Neanderthal, bad ass swings before the door gave up and slunk open.

Zach dropped the hammer and stepped into the house. He headed straight for the painting, following Davey's map.

It felt liberating, like running through an art gallery but with no attendant to chastise him for the sacrilege.

The Japanese Fire Tree hung on a wall in the study behind a desk, whose ebony surface shimmered in the fading light.

Retracing his route, Zach scampered down the stairs and laid the painting in the car's trunk, the dimensions having been confirmed ahead of time.

He jumped into the car, roared it out through the gates, and made a right turn on to the highway.

"Under no circumstance do you come direct to the farm! Make sure you transfer the painting. I don't want no neighbours telling the cops they saw whatever car you used for the robbery turning into Tennessee's farm an hour later. There'll be no cops looking for you after you leave his house. They'll probably respond to the alarm after a few minutes but until Tennessee's wife gets home they won't know what they're looking for, so no speeding. You got lots of time to get to your spot and move the painting to your car. I'll give your girlfriend the money when she gets to the farm and I get the painting. In the meantime, you just get yourself back to town without being stopped."

A couple of hundred yards along, out of sight of the CCTV, Zach turned left onto a dirt road.

He pulled the mask off his face, pitched it out the window, and slowed the car.

Easy peasy. Fade to black.

Zach had only spotted the tractor ruts the day before. They ran off the shoulder of the road and disappeared behind a row of cedar trees. It was a farmer's access route to his back fields.

There was no traffic to watch Zach turn on to the trail.

Blanche was waiting in Zach's Grand Am, hidden from view by the trees. She'd been anxiously wanting to move and to see that Zach was safe.

Zach crept the car past the Grand Am and stopped the Eclipse with their trunks aligned. As he got out, the lids were simultaneously drifting upwards.

Zach quickly transferred *The Japanese Fire Tree* from one car to the other.

After he slammed shut the trunk of the Grand Am, Blanche stuck her head out of the driver's side window and said impatiently, "Can I go now?"

While she waited, she'd been thinking once more of all the reasons that she disapproved of what they were doing. She was angry with herself for not saying "no" to the scheme, and she was blaming Zach for her self-recrimination.

Zach recognized the edge. He'd rolled over her objections to the robbery as if they were nonsense. He always justified such behaviour by telling himself that once Blanche thought something that it became reality. That there was no dissuading her of it so talk was useless, one could only force another version of the facts upon her (confirming Blanche's view that controlling reality was the basis of power).

Acting more nonchalant than he felt, Zach walked to Blanche's window, ducked down to look at her, and said, "Take your time. No speeding tickets to leave a trace. Just act naturally. After the cops watch the CCTV they'll be looking for a man in an Eclipse."

Blanche's response was to gun the engine and stare at Zach in a way that dared him to criticize the act.

The Grand Am leaped forward, skidded around the end of the island of trees and then again when Blanche turned on to the dirt road.

Zach shook his head at the sound of the car's motor quickly fading in volume. She's pissed off, he rationalized, but this was going to help her in the end. She'd calm down.

He turned towards the field. It would be a mile walk along the tractor trail to the nearest town where he would catch the bus back to the city. It was already dark enough that no one would spot him if they happened to look out over the field. As he set off, he smiled at how well things had gone.

Police Trooper Davis, judging from the movement of the headlights ahead, reckoned the vehicle had blown past the stop sign at the intersection of the dirt side road and the highway. She'd heard of the Ross mansion alarm over the radio. A possible robbery. And while it wasn't her call, the behaviour of the driver ahead was certainly suspicious enough to suggest a possible connection.

Davis sped up and got close enough to the Grand Am to make out the plate. She ran it. Clean. But there was still sufficient reason for a stop and search. Davis turned on the overhead.

The Grand Am was obediently pulled to the shoulder. Before exiting the cruiser, Davis was on the radio asking for back up. She'd stopped a vehicle that had sped through a stop sign a few minutes from a probable robbery. And the car was moving in a direction going away from the Ross mansion.

11.

James Ross picked up his iPhone, in its bejeweled case, that had been laying at the ready by his right hand and took a call from the security company monitoring his house.

Ruby poked at her meatloaf. She didn't much like meatloaf but James had ordered for the both of them as he always did. She took up her own designer phone from the table and did a quick check for messages – none of interest – so she studied James' face as he listened to his caller.

It revealed nothing of the nature of his call. He flatly said, "When?" and "How?" and added that he'd be home soon.

"Is everything okay?" Ruby said when James signed off. His words, not his tone, were cause for concern.

"That was my security company. They said there appears to have been a break in at the house."

With a sharp intake of breath, Ruby said, "Your art! Did they say what was taken? We'd better go."

"Yes, yes, we better. I'm finished my meatloaf anyway."

"The right of the common man to a good life is interpreted as the right of a few exceptional individuals, say one in a thousand – or less – to exploit the resources of a new continent in such a way as to make themselves inordinately rich. When I say 'exceptional' I do not wish to be understood as meaning that they are superior. In every other relationship of life besides the making of money they may be, and quite often are, inferior. But as the nineteenth century proceeded on this continent, they were the ones who ran away with your political myth, and with them it degenerated into the false and vulgar idea that anybody in America could get rich if he were willing to set his mind to it. In this present century [20th] you are having to rescue the original conceptions of your political myth from those few individuals controlling corporate wealth who falsified it."
– Alfred North Whitehead, The Dialogues of Alfred North Whitehead

12.

The trail Zach followed was the source of numerous stumbles because it was nothing more than two tractor ruts over roots, and rocks. He couldn't see his own feet and was simply following a silhouetted farmer's path, its contours wavering in the wind and disappearing with each cloud that blocked the moon. And then there were the demon mosquitoes. Since they couldn't be seen, reaction to them was only effective in enacting revenge. By the time he got to the bus depot in the nearest town, he had numerous splotches of blood on his neck and the backs of his hands.

Back in the city, Zach crossed the street where the

Greyhound had dropped him and caught a local bus.

In the seat in front of Zach, two women were talking about a film they'd just seen; which engaged his attention.

In the seat behind him, an older man was telling his companion that a homeless man visible outside the window was a bully named Bernie, who he'd gone to school with.

Across the aisle from Zach, a young couple who'd just gotten on the bus were taking their seats.

"So what's that you were saying about Japan?" said one of the men as they settled.

"I was just reading an online news story, about the arrest of some woman near Kain. She stole some Japanese painting worth millions of dollars. Owned by one of the Ross clan, of course."

"So they got the painting back then, too bad."

Zach was struck by the fact that certain parts of the conversation – "stolen painting", "Japanese" – echoed what he'd just been doing. Quite a coincidence. He smiled.

Realization that the stolen painting must be *The Japanese Fire Tree* came abruptly and triggered his first anxiety attack in sixteen months. He began the cognitive exercises learned during suicide watch in the psych ward. Deep breathing, slow exhale, clenched legs since he was in no position to do squats, cheek against the bus window to simulate an icy splash to the face or the cold shower kicking in after your minutes of hot water were done. And the mental exercises that began by assuming the worst and living through it. Like a pain killer had been shot into a vein, relief spread throughout his body.

His level of blind faith and ignorance suddenly struck him with force and he heaped scorn on himself. How could he have been so stupid as to not realize that the art wasn't some worthless piece of sappy crap done by Aunt Millicent? Plus the house was way beyond the means of Tennessee Butler. The security system alone must have cost ten grand and the place was an art gallery. You don't hang junk in a house like that, with expensive art on the walls. And it wasn't just the discoveries he made at the house that should have alerted him. There were lots of clues beforehand. Who'd go to the trouble of a court order to keep a worthless painting? Or pay someone two grand to steal it? Fuck. Fuck. And double fuck.

Because of his arrogance and stupidity, Blanche was in serious trouble and looking at major jail time. Well, he'd get Davey and they'd go to the cops. Blanche would soon be out.

13.

Davey punched at the TV remote to switch off the Ross news channel, jumped to his feet, swore, and stalked out of the room, as if not being in the presence of the television and his cell phone would help.

The flickering cave shadows played out on the TV screen as Davey paced back and forth in his filthy kitchen. The TV show was (of all things!) an early episode of *Conor and Biddy*, Zach's short-lived cable series, locally shot with local talent, but set in an unnamed northern American city in 1848 among the Irish refugees who'd fled the potato famine. Zach was lilting in his unique, Dublin by way of the Washington Avenue Actors Academy accent.

The episode synthesized actual historical incidents where the established Protestants ran their Orange parades through Catholic areas filled with recent refugees who'd fled the potato famine and managed to dodge the cholera rampant on the ships. The Protestants paraded, armed with guns and axes, knowing they'd be exonerated for their murders and maiming of people who they saw as a threat.

The writers portrayed the Protestants as a group with scant privilege and advantage, so easily stirred to fears of losing the little they had by Irish Protestant leaders who thought that they were part of the ruling English elite, not realizing that they were being used by them. Then, as now, religion was appropriated by a cause to make it appear that it was being defended by standing up for the privilege of the wealthy. Violence and killing ramps up when it's done in god's name.

The episode, unintentionally perhaps given the air date, provided a neat parallel with the current nativism, bigotry, and violence directed towards refugees and those of other religions by people thinking that this advanced their interests.

In the episode playing out, the Orangeman Conor had been knocked unconscious by a thrown stone and rather than let her Catholic countrymen and women get to him, Biddy had dragged him into her house, and revived him.

> **Cut to: Conor**, who struggles to sit, with **Biddy** placing her hand on his back, bending over and helping him.
>
> **Cut to: Biddy**, who kneels, reaches down to

the floor to pick up a piece of cloth that she has set there. She tears a strip off the cloth and begins to wrap **Conor's** head.

Cut to: Conor.

Conor

If I leave and try to walk down the street I may not survive.

Biddy

And you won't survive if you stay here. There's a back door. The privy is at back of the yard with a shelter for wood beside it. Lay behind that, out of sight, and wait for dark. (Standing up.) We must go!

Cut to: Conor getting up with help, shakily. **Biddy** lets go of him, bends, picks up the wrapping cloth and wipes the floor.

Cut to: Conor being assisted along the **hall of the small house** by **Biddy**.

Conor

Why are you helping me?

Biddy

I don't know why I should. You're a bunch of murderers, criminals with guns who come to our part of town with your sorrowful parade to provoke and kill. And you call yourself "protectors" of a country that regards all Irish as dirt, they same way they see former slaves; and you think you have some power. They want you to blame Catholics for your miseries and see us as threats to what you have, all so you don't blame them, the men of power, the real culprits. I know you have rage but you have the wrong people in your sights … Still, if I don't help you I'm no better I suppose.

Cut to: Conor and **Biddy** emerging from the **back door** of the house. In the background, once outside, we can again hear noises from the July 12th march, now in the distance: the slow ominous beat of the lambegs, the yells of the Catholic residents, Protestants chanting "Croppies lie down", then a rifle shot followed by screaming.

Cut to: **Biddy**'s face turning as she hears her **father**'s voice from inside the house calling her name.

Biddy

(urgently to Conor) Go nigh!

Cut to: **Biddy**, seen from inside the house as she steps through the **back doorway** and closes the door behind her. She stops, looking up towards the camera.

Cut to: Biddy's father **Michael** standing at the other end of the **hall** looking at Biddy.

Michael

Ah, there you are.

Fade to black.

Fade in: **Biddy** emerges from the **back door** of the house and quickly moves across the **yard** looking about. It is now dark and since it is 3:00 a.m. it is also quiet.

Cut to: **Conor**, who is asleep behind the **outhouse**. Biddy wakens him by shaking his shoulder. He opens his eyes. Somewhere through the fog he becomes aware of a woman's voice speaking to him. When he opens his mouth to speak she shushes him. He sits up. **Biddy** holds out a glass of water which **Conor** takes and drinks greedily from.

Biddy

You must go. Head that way (pointing). Stay out of the street until you get to the next road and then go left.

Conor

What's your name?

Biddy

It doesn't matter.

Cut to: **Conor** climbs to his feet, starts to go, then turns to look at **Biddy**. He stares.

Cut to: Biddy who stares back. Eventually …

Biddy

Biddy

Biddy turns and hustles towards the house.

Davey wandered back into the room with the TV, noticed Conor/Zach on the screen, shook his head and muttered aloud, "You dumb fucking dickhead. And your Irish accent is pathetic. No wonder your shit show got axed."

Davey's cell rang. He started, then trudged to the coffee table to pick up the phone.

"So what the hell happened?" the caller said.

"I have no idea, yet, but I'm working on it."

"Do you have any idea of how much money was just flushed down the toilet because of that woman? I'll tell you. Five million dollars ransom money from the insurance company. And what's your pretty boy TV star have to say for himself? What a fucking loser. I knew he was gonna screw up."

"Zach's okay. We go back a long time. I haven't heard from him yet. He's probably still on the bus, on his way home. Maybe the cops did random car searches because of the robbery. It's what we were afraid of. I won't know til I talk to him. … Can we try this again?"

"Again? Are you a fucking idiot? No! The insurance will go through the roof and the painting will probably have to be guarded like Fort Knox. It'll be going into storage. We just have to move on to phase two."

"Yeah. It's not over."

"That doesn't matter. Your two dickheads just cost me five million. Fuck!"

Davey sat down and thought. He phoned Tennessee. His sense of self-preservation had told him that there was nothing to be gained by talking to Zach.

> *"We are no longer in the society of the spectacle ... TV watches us."*
> *– Jean Baudrillard, Simulations*

14.

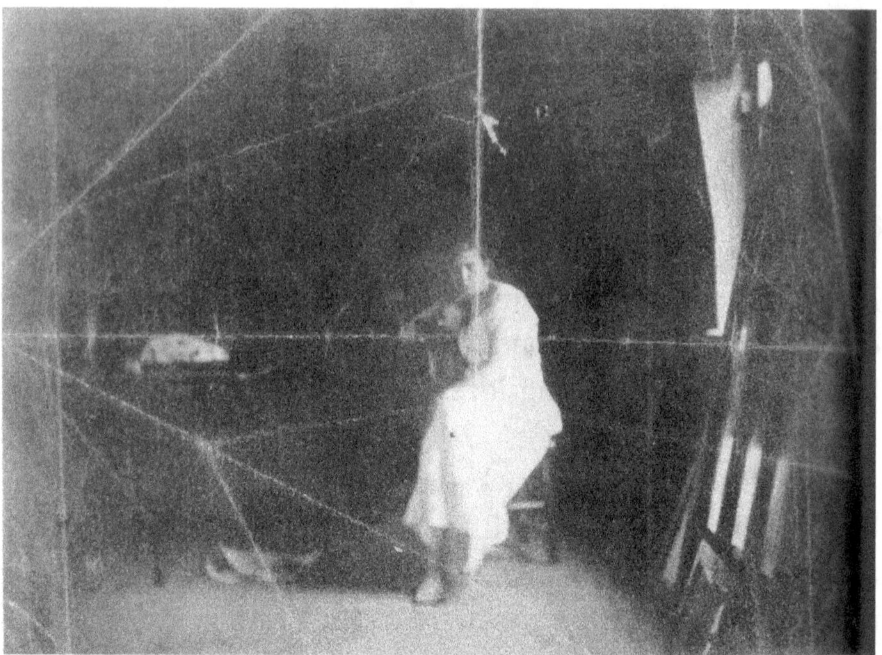

For the third time in the past hour Zach phoned Davey. He needed to be active and wanted to resolve matters as quickly as possible. Once again the call went to voicemail.

In the fantasy reel now looping through Zach's thoughts, keeping his anxiety at bay and comforting him, Blanche was holding strong in jail, accustomed as she was to tough times and knowing that things would soon be sorted out. She was demanding a lawyer in a fiery tone.

Blanche's reality, however, shared little with this cable TV melodrama.

She was being held in a cell at the Kain police station. and hadn't yet been formally charged or even questioned. She looked at the bars of the cell and quickly diverted her eyes.

There's nothing to worry about, she told herself again. The police will figure it out. What had she and Zach really done after all? Taken a man's goods from his own house, at his request. That's it. A big nothing. A fake robbery.

Once she explained to the police and they called Davey or Tennessee Butler the doors would open and she'd be on her way.

And besides, she hadn't even staged the robbery. She was just a delivery person.

Blanche looked down at her hands which, in spite of her self-assurances, were shaking badly and she clenched them. Her experiences with the police when she'd lived down south had been of the worst sort and the very idea of having to deal with an unstoppable and blind authority was terrifying, no matter the circumstances. She leaned her head back against the concrete block wall, closed her eyes, and willed a warm ocean breeze to feather over her face where she lay on a Hawaiian beach.

It was three years since she'd been in a prison.

there is no such thing as radical art

PART 2

"... the most beautiful eyes come from a lifetime of looking people straight in the face ..."
– Antonine Maillet, Evangeline the Second: A Play

15.

Keith was a watcher and an aspiring photo-journalist. He scanned the narrow street below. Nothing. A young woman eventually went past; a woman with the facial features of a girl, briefly illuminated as she walked through a puddle of light. Keith watched her with a growing sense of fatalism and adrenaline-fueled alarm. He looked at women like this as delicate flowers, susceptible to men who would destroy them.

It was unfortunate, he thought, that he wasn't upstairs in his own condo unit where he had a camera mounted at the front window. It would have made a lovely photo, contrasting light and dark.

Hanging on his walls were famous noir photos from the 1940's and the 1950's of people bathed in shadow, with dark insinuation, reflecting the possibly sinister minds of strangers, be they the dreaded Reds, spies, or displaced people without community. Noir reflected the end of certainty about identity and the real.

His favorite photographic subject was women. They were never interactive subjects. The women were always at a distance, often in shadow, usually shot from behind. Iconic, without specific personality. The distance spoke of his isolation but also reflected unsatisfied desire and longing. And loneliness.

"Do you have a choice in who you love?" Sarah asked him on that spring day – it was three years ago now – *"Or is it something that just happens?"*

The two of them were soldiers stationed in Afghanistan. Keith had been returning to barracks from guard duty, rifle still in hand, when Sarah demanded he wait. She stood in his path, facing him. She was having this out with him.

"Why?" he replied.

"Cus I love you and I didn't have a choice."

Embarrassed, surprised, uncertain of his own feelings, and withering in her gaze, Keith looked down at the sand. Sarah had been moving towards this moment he suddenly realized.

Should I have lied and said I loved her too? he now wondered. I could have in time.

Two male soldiers walked by, swapping stories, their laughter splintering the silence.

Sarah and Keith avoided looking at the passing soldiers who headed to a large metal shed nearby. As they were going through the door, one called back, with mocking seductiveness, "Can you give us a hand Sarah?"

The other soldier laughed at the double entendre.

Sarah looked up, said, "Sure," and followed them into the shed.

The door closed behind her.

Keith stood, staring at the shed, wanting to reach out and draw Sarah back.

He became increasingly anxious. He had seen soldiers who'd been intentionally stripped of even basic humanity by their service, where every depravity is justified.

Keith strode to the door of the shed and flung it open.

Sarah was standing twenty feet from the door, a smiling soldier on each side of her, one of them lightly holding her left arm. His partner was telling a story. The three of them simultaneously looked over at Keith.

"You okay Sarah?" Keith said.

"Everything's under control sir," one of the men answered, with a mock salute.

Sarah turned her face away from Keith.

"Leave her alone," Keith said.

"Go away hero," said the story-teller. "We're not holding her."

"Hero," repeated the other man, laughing, as if the word itself was a good joke, or maybe he said, "nothing to worry

about." Frankly I don't recall what I was told that he said.

Keith raised his rifle and pointed it at the latter speaker. "I will shoot you if you don't let go of her."

The man didn't move.

"And what proof did I have that they were a threat, engaged in the early stages of some sort of assault?" Keith would say, later, in the PTSD group where he met Blanche and Stella. "It could have been alleged that I was just a jealous lover if they knew about the recent conversation I'd had with Sarah."

Keith aimed and fired his rifle.

The soldier to his right was struck in the left leg. He yelped and buckled, clutching his calve.

The other guy, shouted, "Jesus!" He advanced a single step towards Keith.

Keith, shifted his rifle. Aimed.

The man stopped.

"Kneel down!" Keith yelled.

The soldier complied. Desperate, primal, fixed eyes.

Keith took a stride forward and spectacularly booted the kneeling soldier in the face.

The man flipped up, like a doll, and came down on his side. He contracted into a fetal position, arms covering his head, as if blindness would make it all unreal.

Keith looked at Sarah and tried to speak. "I … I thought … I thought that …" The words staggered like they were drunk, and then fell down. "Oh fuck it," he said.

Sarah never went to see Keith in the prison or the hospital. Nor did she come here to the city to see him after he was released.

Keith's condo unit was one floor above the one where he now stood, across the hall from mine, and one floor below Blanche's. This two-bedroom flat was home to his friend Cindy and her thirteen year old daughter Cheryl.

At the time that he bought his own unit, Keith wondered what it was that he owned since he didn't own the physical structure itself. It felt like he'd just purchased the space inside, a concept that struck him as extremely odd, perhaps the way the idea of owning land had apparently sounded to native people.

In the end, he decided that what he'd actually purchased was perspective and distance; a means to escape the city and observe it from above. To study it as one would a specimen.

The city below, he thought, was a dreary and unattractive area, and ugliness, as the Romantics knew, as children do, is an aesthetic judgment that is the first incarnation and validation of an intellectual critique. Ugliness indicates that an enterprise is built on greed and commerce, and in opposition to nature and community. The city was a reflection of the obscenity of modern America, where in spite of being the wealthiest country in the history of the world, millions of people live in abject poverty and without hope of ever knowing a better life.

The building where he lived was an old warehouse that had been converted into somewhat fashionable condos. Until recently, this neighbourhood had housed many poor artists.

Conversely, the grand houses that were once home to the factory and warehouse owners, had been divided into multiple rental units for students, poor people, and seasonal workers. Keith had lived in both parts of the city and felt less a part of it here than when he was homeless.

Still, the condo was his sole consolation for this isolation; to have a space of his own to at least watch the world.

Sometimes, to his credit, Keith would photograph a street scene that captured the life and energy of normal human interaction. Life was fascinating to watch. But even here, his photos reflected the photographer's otherness.

Cindy got up off the couch to head for the kitchen when her cell rang. She answered it, keeping her voice low because Cheryl was asleep.

Keith couldn't make out many of the words but was fairly certain it was the same man who Cindy said had phoned the last three nights. A guy who'd been one of her crowd at high school. He'd apparently developed the curious idea that there had always been some chemistry and intention between the two of them but it had been thwarted by others.

"What's the matter with the guy?" Keith asked when told about him. "Was he always such a creep?"

"He's not a creep. He's just lonely."

"That sounds like more than just loneliness. More like he's a delusional stalker."

"Yes. No. We're all delusional sometimes, aren't we? We don't know what others think or feel. And don't we all turn into creeps when we're rejected, searching people online, watching their Facebook page? We're all stalkers."

Cindy had found her way into the livingroom and held out her cell for Keith, her expression beseeching help.

Keith got up and took it. "Hello," he said in his huskiest pretend-boyfriend voice, "Cindy isn't available, sorry."

Cindy stood watching.

"I want to talk to Cindy," the caller said.

"Sorry," said Keith. "Can you please let this go?"

The man on the line said, more insistently this time, his

voice rising in a half cry, "I want to talk to Cindy."

"Cindy doesn't want to talk about this, good-night."

As Keith took the phone from his ear, the man wailed, "I want to talk to Cindy!" A wrenching plea as if part of him was being torn away.

Keith pressed the cell's screen to end the call and passed the phone to Cindy.

On her way back to the kitchen Cindy jumped when it began to ring. She let it continue until it went to message, set it on the table and was on her way to her bedroom when it rang again. She returned to the kitchen and this time switched the phone off.

Keith arose, went to the front window and scanned the street below wondering if the caller was out front. He was worried that the guy might be on his way up to the unit. Perhaps he'd come walking down the street in a few minutes.

A short time later, Keith headed back to his place and to bed. He began to relax as soon as he left Cindy's.

"It's a really important part of the radical tradition to be able to say that one of the things wrong with capitalism in general is that it produces a certain kind of aesthetic degradation says [Jeremy Gilbert]. 'And that does speak to something that really intuitively people recognise – not just aesthetes, not just intellectuals. Most people have a sense of the way in which corporate culture cannot produce beauty. It can appropriate it and sell access to it, but it can't produce it.'"
– Larry Ryan, 'Ruskin the radical: why the Victorian thinker is back with a vengeance'

16.

Stella looked around the shop. Stella's Bakery. Her bakery. It was more than closed. It was empty, cleaned out except for the shelves and some personal items in one corner.

The realization of this moment as the end of one of the aspirations of her life brought a visceral sense of anxiety, as if a death had occurred. This was followed by a flash of resentment at James Ross III who'd murdered her dream; the expected end for people who opposed the Ross family.

Stella stepped outside to check on the effectiveness of her efforts to cover the windows with brown craft paper. Now opaque, they reflected a lone car and its watching driver slowly passing behind her, elongating then compressing, as if being seen in a distorting mirror at the fair. There was no window sign giving her forwarding address, just a thank-you note to her loyal customers, positioned between the graffiti.

If she had looked through the shop's window during the daytime, as recently as two weeks earlier, baking would have been visible through the window, sitting in baskets on pine shelves. Sweet potato and banana-pecan muffins, flourless brownies, millet and buckwheat bread, almond cranberry tea biscuits, granola cookies, apple-cinnamon pie, zucchini nut cake.

Tonight would be the final one in her apartment downstairs. Most of her things were now stacked in the bakery. Likely, this would soon be her home.

17.

In Cheryl's dream she was out walking under the streetlights along a road that ran beside a park. She came upon a man's head where it rested on the cement sidewalk. It was a detached head, so no body or limbs obviously.

The head said, "Hello," and tried to strike up a conversation about the weather.

When Cheryl mentioned that she was tired because she'd played soccer earlier earlier that evening, the head launched into a story about his own brilliance on the soccer pitch. He didn't stop there but went on to elaborate with examples and Cheryl had to listen to several stories out of politeness.

The head was an incredibly gifted soccer player the way he told it.

He said, "If I was in a phone booth with three men and a soccer ball I could control the ball and dribble my way through the crowd."

That's very unlikely, Cheryl thought, he's a disembodied head after all.

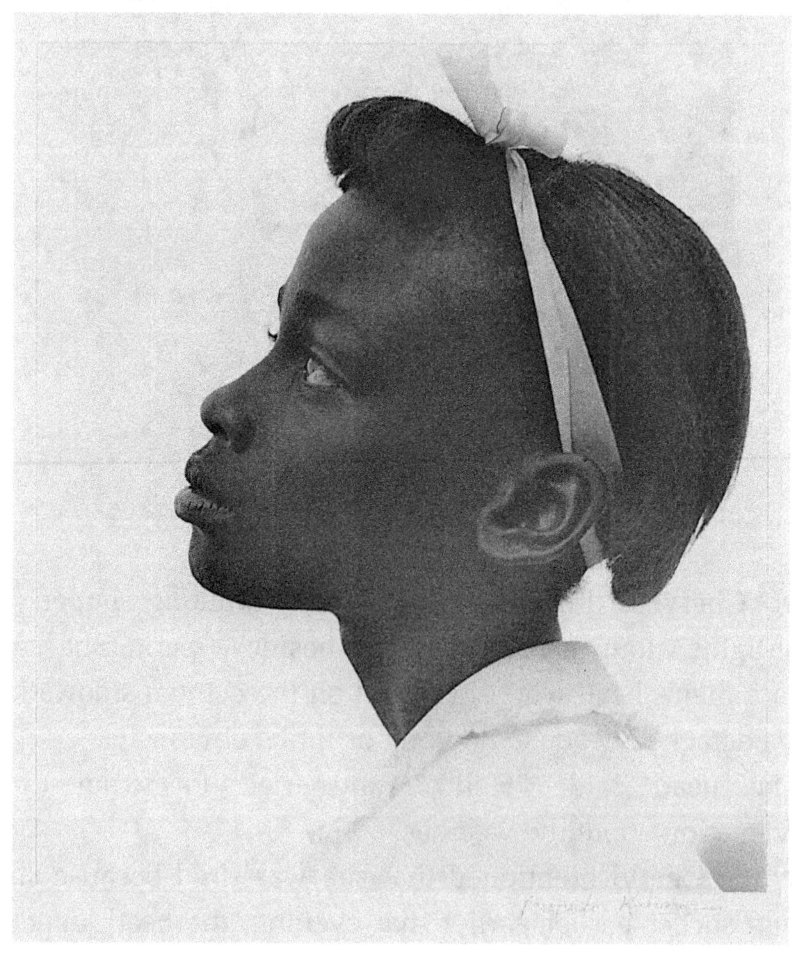

18.

At 7 a.m., Keith walked downstairs to Cindy's condo.

In a rapid fire staccato, Cindy, standing at the open door, said, "Cheryl's in the shower, call me anytime, if need be, and thanks." She then brushed past Keith, heading for the airport, and a week-long work conference.

Keith had agreed to drive Cheryl to her father's place, where she'd stay the week. Cindy didn't like the idea of Cheryl staying there or traveling across the city on her own.

Keith sat in the livingroom with a cup of coffee waiting for Cheryl to finish her shower. He heard the water shut off.

Soon, wearing only a bath towel wrapped around her, her damp hair hanging loose, Cheryl opened the bathroom door, nonchalantly walked to her bedroom, and closed the door. Her mother would have been shocked at this lack of shyness from a thirteen year old girl, Keith knew. Cindy had stood opened mouthed the evening before when Cheryl walked through the kitchen, in front of Keith, wearing only underwear and a t-shirt.

Cheryl in her towel, Keith thought, seemed to be imitating the type of titillating voyeur pleasing scene you might see in an old movie, or some other puritanized version of the multi-cultural, centuries-old artistic depictions of seductive and beautiful bathing women, nymphs, oreads, mermaids, selkies, hulder, sirens or succubus, leading men to destruction by looking, women slaying them for their gaze.

This wasn't a Lolita moment for Keith. He remembered many years before when his younger sister, also at age thirteen, after months of being very uncomfortable with the new experience of men looking at her and complaining to their mother about it, began to mimic scenes of female seductiveness from movies she'd seen. She did this when their uncle was around.

Keith didn't think that his sister and Cheryl were actually trying to seduce men, but were simply taking on roles to try out adult behaviour, as we all do.

He couldn't articulate precisely why but he still felt a certain uneasy confusion. Perhaps, because the girls were mimicking images of women made to satisfy the male gaze; perhaps assuming that male fantasy was reality. He was unsure if they were conforming themselves to this view of women – as ultimately objects of the male gaze – or trying to gain control of such a world. Or both.

In any case, he thought that Cheryl was acting out these roles in front of him, practicing being looked at with him, because she perceived him as safe. He felt no certainty about any of this, but females had indeed always seen him as safe.

"Telling our stories matters now more than ever. We live in an age of intense loneliness and social isolation, a lack of community, and constant anxiety. This is on top of our natural solipsism, where the only reality we know with certainty is inside our heads. By telling our own stories we reach out to the world.

When we imagine ourselves in the skin of others or listen to the stories of others, we are forced to see the world from different perspectives, gaining in empathy and understanding, and recognizing human connections and dignity. We combat the constant vilification of others based on factors like skin color, religion, gender, ethnicity, sexual preference, class, and ability. And we come to appreciate others as people who suffer, and who love.

We are immersed in self-serving corporate media productions that seldom reflect the reality of the lives of many; particularly excluding the stories of older women, people of color, and those that polite society looks down on. They promote myths of American exceptionalism and benevolence, military glory, and the idea that we live in a meritocracy; all the while churning out endless remakes of super hero movies and turning others into cartoon villains.

Most of us are silent and live in the shadows, but by telling our stories we can honestly shine a light on the world around us and forge myths that glorify compassion, moral responsibility, honesty, and integrity."

– Eléonore Brunette, Under the Porch Light

19.

In the warehouse where she was squatting, laying on a mattress on the floor, Belle Brooks flicked off her tiny battery powered TV and rolled on to her back, cocked an arm under her head and stared up at the steel beams in thought. She'd just listened to a news piece about the theft of a Schiele painting and was curious about it, wondering, assuming even, that there was something crooked about the whole affair, quite apart from the theft itself. It had that feel.

She'd never seen *The Japanese Fire Tree* and hoped there'd be a photo of it in the press. While in art college, she'd looked at some of Schiele's work, found it interesting, and radical if you considered the time period. It seemed to her that Schiele had primarily been attempting to depict human intimacy in its boldest terms – an embrace, the explicit display of sex organs, masturbation, lesbian and heterosexual sex, familial love – eschewing conventional beauty and idealist clichés in favor of the rawness and even ugliness of active, real people.

She wondered if Schiele envisioned a social role for his art in overcoming repression. It was Freud's Vienna after all. Now, several years later, she thought that while Schiele's radicalism likely had some effect, radicalism, as her friend Donal McGraith said, was always recuperated. Schiele's work now hung ineffectually on the walls of the wealthiest, and in galleries (or more likely, packed in some crate in the storage facilities they employed because of exorbitant insurance premiums; an outcome of seeing art as a scarce commodity). The art market tamed every radical impulse, in the end, by containing it. Every artist's cry for humanity was turned into a commodity as poor compensation for life stripped of  passion and intimacy. There is no such thing as radical art.

All art, she felt, is dead even as it celebrates and proclaims life. Just as her words attacking art always fell dead from her lips the moment she said them. Just as her art died when she put it on a canvas.

(Donal McGraith was a local writer who criticized the two primary intellectual ideas that were the foundation of the art market and the academia which sustains it: originality and authenticity. Originality leads to the belief that valuable artworks are unique works of rare genius, and sustains the speculative art market's contention that it is dealing in rare commodities only discernible by the expert eye. Which also undermines our belief in the legitimacy of our own creative efforts. Authenticity is the quasi-religious belief that valuable art is akin to sacred objects because they have been touched by the hand of a particular genius; that an artwork's value derives from this so that an identical forgery is worthless although it shares the same aesthetic qualities.)

It was with this in mind that Belle drew only on walls using biodegradable paints knowing her work would quickly disintegrate; refusing to make more useless art commodities (which destroy resources and pollute the environment).

She had no interest in following the route of some other street artists to make commercial copies of her work to sell in galleries, or to move it inside to create permanent pieces. Nor did she accept commissions from companies to create pseudo street art that might enhance their brand. Or create a brand of her own. Or celebrate icons like Che Guevara and Obama.

She refused all monetization of her work by producing anonymously and kept to the original aims of many street artists by challenging consumerism with actions like détourning billboards.

Belle celebrated DIY and beautiful failure. She made street art to reclaim public space as a commons for artistic expression, rejecting the notion that the city was owned by people like the Ross family.

"The erratic progress of desire, the quest for love of the self, the call of adventure – all of these recognise a right to the pleasure resident in the ugly, the flawed, the unaccomplished, the insufficient: this is the pleasure to be found in the sketch, the rough draft, the incongruous brush stroke, the false note ... All human beings have the right to artistic expression."
– Raoul Vaneigen, A Declaration of the Rights of Human Beings

20.

After dropping off Cheryl at her father's, Keith drove downtown to Stella's bakery.

Keith walked down the concrete steps at the side of the bakery leading to Stella's apartment. He looked through the door's window into a vacant space illuminated by a single overhead light. In a Kafkaesque scene, a middle-aged man, was sitting at a wooden desk and plunking away on a laptop.

Keith knocked. The man glanced up and waved him in.

Sticking his face around the door, which he held partially open, Keith asked the man if knew where Stella was.

The guy studied him, making an assessment.

"We're friends," Keith explained.

"Sorry," the man said. "I have no idea. She was here this morning. I even helped lug her futon up to the store. But I have no idea where she is now."

Keith apologized for the intrusion and retreated. He immediately pulled out his cell and dialed Stella's number but got a recorded message saying that the phone number was no longer in service.

He climbed to the sidewalk, undecided about where to go next but eventually headed for the adjacent variety store.

A dour looking woman standing at the counter, arms crossed, looked at him without expression and said in a flat voice, "You have to leave your backpack at the front."

"Oh sorry," Keith said smiling, "I forgot I had it since I don't usually carry it when I come to Stella's."

In the hectoring tone of the deeply offended, the woman said, "You've been here a few times with the backpack on but I've said nothing." She frowned and pulled her sweater closer, as if Keith was a cold draft. The word "Stella" had apparently brought on the frost – it now had that effect on a number of Tribune readers – and there is nothing quite as assured as the ugly and unfeeling response from someone who thinks they have the high moral ground because of a Tribune hit job.

"Ah, sorry."

Keith walked to the row of coolers along the back of the shop, grabbed a bottle of water from one of the fridges, and returned to the front where he set it on the glass that covered the lottery tickets on the counter, beside the cash register. Some condensation immediately dripped on to the glass and formed a tiny puddle.

The woman stared at the water as if beaten down by the slings and arrows of life. She took the bill Keith proffered, thrusting his change back at him without comment; her daggered look dripping its own pool of disdain.

I should have just left, Keith thought after exiting, while walking to a bench in the park across the street from the bakery having decided that Stella would be back soon so he should sit and watch for her.

He held a small camera in one hand, which he twice used to take surreptitious snaps of people around him; scenes of intimacy and thus also alienation, his images making him a tourist even in his home town. Always the outsider.

Keith liked this particular camera because he could operate it discretely. His subjects didn't know they were being photographed since he could hold the camera at waist height and look down into the view finder. A tool to steal intimacy.

Directly in front of him was a purple Tribune newspaper box. On the front page, he could make out a photo of the family reunion of a soldier. The piece sparked Keith's usual anger at what he considered to be military propaganda.

He had no idea, of course, that a story about the theft of *The Japanese Fire Tree* had been squeezed into the bottom half of page one, bumping a photo of the Stars and Stripes flying over the state building, a fact attesting to the robbery's exceptional import.

The Tribune never printed photos showing the devastation, civilian deaths and starvation caused by America's illegal bombings and sanctions. This was censorship. Instead, they promoted a glossy image of the military as all sacrifice and heroism. God was on our side and hated the enemy.

The Orwellian destruction of critical thought and vocabulary in Ross Media and the state's schools fostered the inability of many to think outside of dogma. Words like "freedom" and even "America" had been appropriated by conservatives to the extent that, for some, their very utterance affirmed conservative dogma as actual historic American values and to dissent from these was traitorous. People cheered for tax dollars going, not to help them, but to support military action on behalf of the wealthy, and their kids died "defending America".

Everyone, even leftists, said to the soldiers, "Thank you for your service", as if the soldiers were defending the country by bombing the life out of peasant armies and civilians on the other side of the world in countries which posed no threat to the U.S. but whose resources were wanted by the wealthy. WAR IS PEACE.

He couldn't escape his memories of the murdered and maimed he'd seen. Of the depravities he'd witnessed, committed by both sides.

In spite of his personal view that seeing transforms us he was also aware that it could be temporary and saw no point in lobbying The Tribune for more realism. So, while the photography that never appeared in The Tribune could sway public opinion, the way it did during the Vietnam war, it wouldn't fundamentally change people's view about the rightness of American imperialism or exceptionalism.

Thou shalt not kill (unless they have something we want).

"As many as 576,000 Iraqi children may have died because of economic sanctions imposed by the Security Council. ..."
– Barbara Crossette, 'Iraq Sanctions Kill Children, U.N. Reports.' 1995, NY Times

"When asked on US television if she thought that the death of half a million Iraqi children was a price worth paying, [Madeleine] Albright replied: 'This is a very hard choice, but we think the price is worth it.'"
– John Pilger, 'Squeezed to Death,' 2000, The Guardian

"In September 2006, Albright – along with Václav Havel – received the Menschen in Europa Award for furthering the cause of international understanding."
– Wikipedia, 'Madeleine Albright'

"We in the United States have yet to realize both the futility and immense consequences of war. We continue to develop, store, sell, and use hideous weapons. We rob ourselves and others of resources needed to meet human needs, including grappling with the terrifying realities of climate change. We should heed the words and actions of Eglantyne Jebb, who founded Save the Children a century ago. ... 'Every war,' said Jebb, 'is a war against children.'"
– Kathy Kelly, 'Every War is a War Against Children', 2019, The Progressive

21.

A half hour later, Stella and Keith were in Keith's car on the way to his condo, and to Cindy's, on temporary loan to Stella.

"How are you?" Keith said. "Really."

"I'm fine. Really. The stress level can only go down now that I don't have the yahoos to deal with."

She was referring to the men who would phone her with death and rape threats, and who threw garbage and dead animals at the store. They always acted anonymously, of course, following a cue from their pack leaders since cowards always require a gang and feel particularly brave when the target is a woman. The threat of rape is a way to feel power for cowards and impotent men. It was the tenor of the time, with fascism on the rise, including in the U.S., that gave them the courage to go on the attack.

More than ever this is a world without eye contact where people can operate anonymously.

In her environmental activism against Ross businesses she had to grant that she'd gotten off lighter than reporters from independent journals who were pointed out and then attacked by police, sometimes brutally. Invariably, the police asserted that that the reporters were actually participants so any violence directed against them was there own fault.

"Fucking Tribune," said Keith. "It's because of them that these gutless wonders feel empowered to come slithering up out of their mother's basements."

Stella didn't reply, looking instead to her right, out the window. Her sanguine attitude was due to civility and resignation rather than disagreement.

"How's the science website going?" Keith said.

"It's looking good, but not much in the way of traffic." The website in question was meant to counter The Tribune's monopoly on misinformation regarding such things as pesticides, clear-cutting, the toxic waste from Ross mills and the wildlife deaths they cause. "I suppose that a mass movement might be the best way for things to improve but every small, personal act matters. And information can encourage that. God knows, waving picket signs at a Ross business has no effect; they don't care. I think that we may need to engage in civil disobedience to get attention."

The usual morning activities went on around them. Traffic clustered and slowed. Multiple horns uselessly honked. An occasional cyclist attempted to maneuver between cars and the curb. People stepped over loosely scattered trash on the sidewalk from an overturned bin, possibly the result of overnight drinkers exercising their hidden seditious impulses loosened by alcohol. Sleepy people stood in long queues, waiting for buses, sporting ear buds with dangling wires.

Panhandlers sat cross-legged on the sidewalk, some from the tent city that the police were demolishing at that exact moment to eradicate the criminality of poverty and of not meeting societal expectations of conformity. Stella thought about third-rate people like James Ross III. People who would shrivel up and die if faced with the challenges of these people living on the streets, yet convinced of their own superiority because they'd inherited Daddy's money. And she was reminded again of the power of Ross Media. Not only was Ross ignoring the reality of people suffering in America, but he'd made it his mission to stoke hate for them. They were a testament to the failure of American capitalism. People like James Ross III betray their country and themselves with their silence about their fellow Americans.

Their backs pressed against building walls, escaping the damper concrete where a light rain had fallen earlier, the panhandlers' cans or hats sitting on the sidewalk in front of them caught the loose coins flipped by a surprising number of passersby attesting to a native kindness that persisted in the face of the ugliness of their leaders and media.

In spite of the efforts made to quell it, this was still a culture that valued kindness. Which causes me to wonder if the extensive attempts by Ross Media and similar outfits – to instill the belief that poverty and suffering are self-inflicted from laziness and the rejection of work – is a reflection of the immensity of the task of convincing people to ignore their own humanity and empathy to counter any notion of political responsibility arising.

Sleeping out

Larceny

"As one of the world's wealthiest societies, the US is what [Philip] Alston, [United Nations watchdog on extreme poverty around the world] calls a 'land of stark contrasts.' It is home to one in four of the world's 2,208 billionaires. At the other end of the spectrum, 40 million Americans live in poverty. More than five million eke out an existence amid the kind of absolute deprivation normally associated with the developing world."
– Ed Pilkington, 'Trump's "cruel" measures pushing US inequality to dangerous level, UN warns'

22.

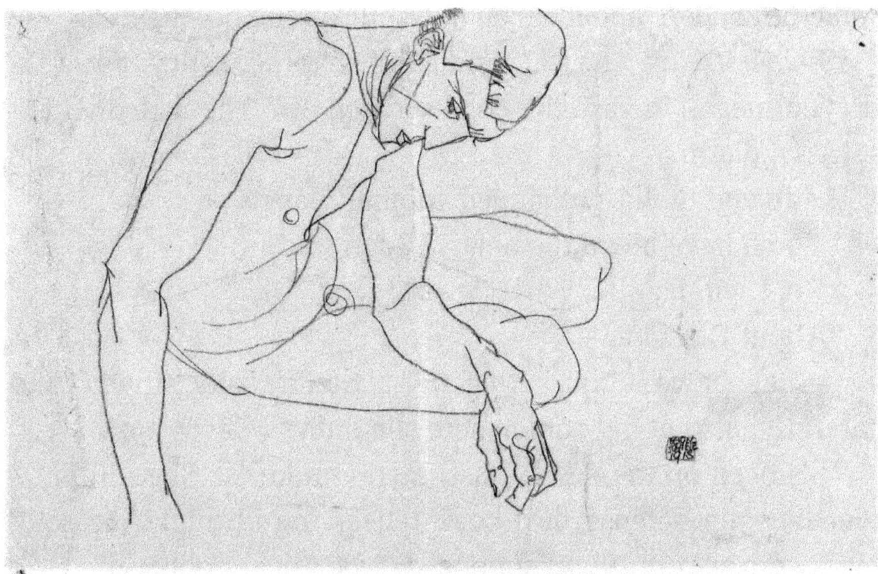

Keith wheeled his car onto the driveway of the condo and drove down a ramp to the underground parking lot where he and Stella decamped, walked to the elevator, and rode it up to his unit to retrieve the key to Cindy's unit for Stella.

Keith had his key in the lock, Stella standing behind him, when they heard a loud whisper, "Keith, Keith, can I come in?"

They turned to see Zach, who was standing in the doorway of the stairwell, holding open the door.

"Are you okay?" asked Keith.

"Yeah, yeah. We need to go inside. Okay?"

"Oh, right. Yes, okay," said Keith, stepping back from the open door and waving Zach inside. He glanced over his shoulder at Stella, who looked back quizzically, her face expressing concern.

Once inside the kitchen, Zach turned to Keith and said, "I spent the night in the stairwell in case the cops showed up. I came down here about seven but you weren't home."

"I was driving Cheryl," said Keith automatically, "but what do you mean, 'In case the cops showed up?'" he added with a sense of alarm.

Keith and Stella exchanged another glance.

"You'll have heard the news," Zach said.

"No," said Keith. "What news?"

"About Blanche."

"What news about Blanche?" Stella said slowly and carefully, also going somewhere she didn't wish to go.

"It's been on the news. I assumed you knew. She's in jail." Pleading the defense he'd been rehearsing all night, he said, "We were set up! It was supposed to be a fake robbery."

"Wait. I'm missing something," said Keith. "The police were here looking for Blanche?"

"No, she was stopped in her car with a stolen painting. A valuable one we were told was of only sentimental value. I think the cops are looking for me. I can't go home."

"Okay, okay, you were involved too." Keith coaxed. "Can you start from the beginning?"

Zach breathed deeply and addressed the court by laying out the facts leading up to the theft of *The Japanese Fire Tree*. He recounted the plan, the apparent lack of risk, and his and Blanche's need for money that made it an enticing enterprise. He didn't mention that Blanche had objections to the scheme. And along the way he interspersed some self-exoneration for the current state of affairs. "I told her to be careful." "I don't know what she did to get herself caught."

"And you're certain that Blanche is in jail because of some

mistake she made?" said Stella. A rhetorical question made for Blanche's defense that went without a response.

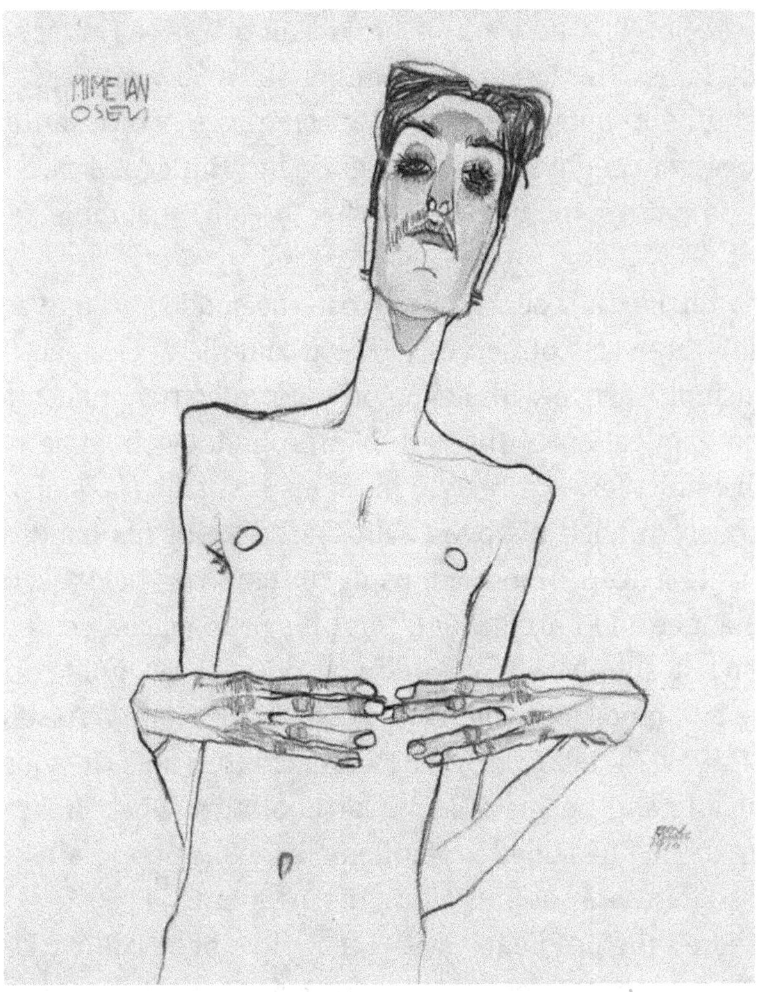

As he paced before the now seated jury, Zach drifted towards the condo window to take in the street below. But like flotsam pushed to shore and then drawn back out to sea by the same wave, he immediately retreated only to again be compelled to return and peek around the drapes. He noted the camera with a telephoto lens, together mounted on a tripod, and his eyes narrowed in a sideways glance at Keith.

Zach went on to explain that the robbery had turned out to be a set up. The house he'd broken into wasn't Butler's, but that of James Ross, and the painting wasn't a worthless piece of sentiment but a European masterpiece worth millions. Blanche got caught taking the painting to Butler's farm.

Stella said something under her breath, inaudible to the others.

The refrigerator began its defrost, the sudden grating sound causing three sets of nerves to react, and the noise then filled the ensuing silence with its melody of proletarian industry.

The explication of his case had brought Zach some peace and he now felt his body's insistent demand for sleep. He vigorously rubbed his eyes with the backs of his hands. His eyes were a deep, blood red, while his skin was pale.

"Blanche and I are fucked," was his pronounced verdict.

"Isn't it simply a matter of you and Davey going to the police and reporting what Butler did?" said Keith. "Assuming that Davey is innocent, and was also set up." It sounded reasonable and businesslike. "Corroborating what Blanche is telling them," he added in implied all caps, a period after each word so there was no mistaking his meaning.

"There's the problem," said Zach. "I've been calling Davey and leaving messages. He finally called me back. Said he didn't know what I was talking about and to leave him alone. Then he hung up."

Keith leaned back on the sofa, looking condemned, feeling the real victim and beseeching the heavens for mercy. "Why does that not surprise me? Is he at home?" He nodded his head in the direction of the front window because Davey lived in a flat across the road. It was how he and Zach had come to run into each other again after so many years.

"Nope. I think he's at Butler's farm. In fact, I suspect he made the phone call to me on Butler's phone since the police are probably listening in on the guy's calls. I know that Butler's behind everything because Blanche was told to take the painting to the farm – and Davey's a gullible simpleton."

"Shit, shit," Stella said in frustration. "Poor Blanche."
"Yes, through Zach's blindness," said Keith, his voice

rising, clearly angry now as he glared at Zach, brandishing his chivalric tool, sculpting Blanche as a victim in need of saving. "Even if the guy's Al Capone, why are you here?"

Zach swallowed his reply. He was in too vulnerable a position to respond in kind.

"Because if they don't believe him then what has he accomplished?" said Stella, always the cooling breeze. "Then they'll both be in jail. The police might even think he set Blanche up."

"Which would at least get her off the hook," said Keith.

"Keith," said Stella. "Keep in mind that Zach's not the villain of the piece here. He was caught in a scam."

"I just think he should do the honorable thing. The cops would look into things. Butler is known to have mob connections so it shouldn't take much convincing that he's up to something shady." Keith's glare went from Zach to Stella as if daring either of them to argue with his moral certainty and faith in police integrity.

"Then they should already be investigating based on what Blanche told them, and if Zach's phone call was heard by the cops then they already know that Zach's confirming whatever Blanche told them," said Stella.

For the next half hour the three discussed their options.

Eventually Zach said to Keith, "Can I get you to drive me to Tennessee's farm? Davey's got to be there … if he's still alive."

"Shit," said Stella sharply. "Do you seriously think that Butler's killed him, or coerced him into silence?"

"Yes."

"Okay, but let's assume he's alive," said Keith. "What are you going to say to him if we find him?"

"We go back a long way. I'll appeal to his better nature."

"If he has one," said Keith. "Plus, he might prefer to shut up rather than betray a guy connected to the mob. It could take a hell of a lot of convincing for him to do that."

"And I also know a lot of stuff about his criminal dealings, his illegal smokes' racket and his drug dealing."

Stella and Keith stared silently at Zach as if seeing him for the first time.

"Well," said Stella. "It's not like we have any other options. And I think you're right to assume that the only way the cops will take you seriously is if you, Davey and Blanche all tell the same story."

After some more back and forth, with Keith still arguing that even with the threat of criminal exposure that Davey might feel safer doing some time for dope dealing than betraying a guy who could have him killed, they all agreed to the plan. To begin after Zach had a nap.

"And what about Blanche?" said Stella. "Where's she? She must be terrified. She'll be needing some support; obviously legal support."

"She might be in Kain Jail," said Zach. "I heard someone say that's where she was arrested."

"If I can use your cell," Stella said, turning towards Keith, "I'll call and check. And if she's there, I'll go and see her."

23.

"You got raccoons up there," pronounced Glover. He spat out the words like they were covered in salt. He didn't like commies, Democrats, northerners, or shit disturbers, and he figured this woman was all four.

Stella looked up towards the roof, but being flat, it wasn't visible from ground level. It was what she'd expected though. This was a small city, and situated at the edge of deep woods, so wildlife regularly wandered into town.

"What I'll do," added Glover, "is put some traps up there. You should check em in the morning and if there's something in any of em call me and I'll come and take the critters to our drop spot."

He proffered something resembling a smile. He budgeted his smiles but knew they were good for business.

Glover's was a catch and release outfit. "Humane pest management", it said on his web page. There was no name on the truck that came round to Stella's bakery, as a courtesy.

"So you'll release them?" Stella confirmed.

"Yeah, and any mice we get in the traps too. What about rats? Same thing?"

"Rats? There's no rats." The idea was a gross one. "Eww. Whatever." Stella laughed.

Stella owned a hearth bakery; the culmination of many fantasies over the years, funded by a small inheritance and all of her savings.

Stella had once been quoted, in an article in The Tribune, criticizing clear-cutting. She was interviewed at a protest of Ross Pulp and Paper about what they were doing in the nearby forests.

There had been no less than fifteen groups over the years that had challenged the Ross company's application of toxic herbicides after its clear-cutting in an effort to destroy trees and plants of no commercial value; transforming the wilderness into commodities. Since their use of the chemicals began there had been a spike in human cancer rates wherever they'd been applied near human habitation and the

wild food plants that survived were poisoned. The Ross company had used their news outlets and lawsuits to turn themselves into victims and the protesters into criminals.

A steady stream of heavy trucks drove in and out of the area day and night to haul trees to their mills and pulp paper facility, a site notorious for its noxious emissions, and its toxic effluent that had led to the destruction of the fisheries of the First Nations' population. Millions of dollars in public money and resources had been poured into the company and public protections obliterated as so much "red tape" while the Ross family off-shored their wealth and paid no taxes. All of the above without local press coverage.

Stella's clear-cut protest, however, had managed to close the major highway for a significant part of the day so The Tribune made an exception and explained the cause of the "nuisance". It was presented as a traffic story.

After that The Tribune called Stella on the rare occasions when it wanted an opposing viewpoint on certain local issues if it acknowledged there was any opposition. A sentence or two from an "activist" to present the image of balanced reporting. This was always followed by a company talking head who told readers and viewers that the protesters were people who wanted to steal their livelihood "to advance their liberal agenda".

Since the clear-cutting protest had focused on the disruption to the local ecosystem and endangered wildlife, Stella was particularly called on to comment on issues involving wild animals and birds in the area. She became the token bleeding heart liberal animal activist.

Stella climbed her step ladder the next morning. There were raccoons in all three cages.

She called Glover who promised to be there at ten a.m. but failed to show.

She called him again in the afternoon. The raccoons were trapped in the hot sun. Still no sign of him.

Called him again after dinner.

Glover came at eight that night and emptied the traps.

Two days later there was an editorial in The Tribune. It was an attack on "outsiders" who'd "recently" moved to the area and were now leading protests. They didn't understand that people's livelihoods depended on local resource industries and resources. The last thing the city needed was for potential tourists, hunters and fishermen, to be reading that the forests were poison, causing them to think twice about visiting and spending their money in the area. Plus, people might worry that they'd have to deal with an "angry mob" when they got there. Those who staged local protests had legal avenues they could use to raise concerns instead of using their "shrill voices".

"Spokespeople" — Stella was mentioned by name — should stop "seeking attention" the editorial also asserted. It added that Stella's personal integrity was lacking. Apparently she'd advised an animal control expert to kill the rats in and around her shop. Unnecessary, when humane animal control was available.

It was only an "alleged incident", but everyone knew that this meant "guilty". It was in the paper after all, and the incident had been mentioned the evening before at a Council meeting, brought up by City Councilor Luke Wallace. He was the brother of Glover the animal control guy, and he was an employee of Ross Mill which had funded his campaign.

The editorial didn't assess Stella's criticisms of the Ross businesses. There was no point. They came from a "self-serving hypocrite" so were invalid. It was an approach as old as Ibsen's 'Enemy of the People' and as recent as the dismissal of environmental activists for their use of airplanes, roads or electricity.

"You've got to respond, Stella," her friend Kathy had insisted in the bakery the day after the editorial appeared. "Call them and tell them the allegations are untrue. Write a letter. Set the record straight. The redneck pig-fuckers

around here will believe anything."

That was going too far. But in spite of that, Stella both wrote to and phoned the paper. Nothing appeared in the newspaper. She was just yelling into the wind.

Over the next weeks, the bakery's business declined.

Some likely thought the premises had a rat infestation.

Some students who felt important having a red hot grudge took to shaming Stella on social media.

Some on the impotent left avoided her thinking that political change began with getting favorable comment in the Ross Media and didn't want to be associated with her.

Some males left death and rape threats on her phone because they were impotent cowards.

Some conservatives were happy that her voice had been silenced. Some working people did as well. Industrialism, and even unionism, were at odds with science since it threatened their incomes, so blindness to facts was an agreed option.

Some of the stupider residents even believed that she was part of some sort of Chinese plot.

Stella became angrier over time but felt powerless.

"It's bloody unfair. I was doing something good when I protested," she told Kathy. "If I could take back what I said to Glover I would, but I shouldn't have to. I didn't tell him to kill anything."

She knew that she was losing the business she'd worked much of her life to have.

A few, who couldn't care less about what had been written in The Tribune, kept going to the bakery. And Stella, in turn, kept putting out her baskets of baking on the pine shelves in the window, all the while knowing that much of it wouldn't sell and would end up going to the local food bank. It was only a matter of time.

After months of losses, keeping the bakery open became impossible. Stella had no savings left.

On her final day of business, after everything inside was cleaned up and spotless, Stella's final act was to wash off the graffiti that had been painted on the shop window during the night for the umpteenth time. The word "hippocrite" (sic) in large letters.

24.

Keith drove his silver Civic through the area of condos. Poor artists had once squatted there and taken over the run down shops and industrial spaces. Of course, artists are the realtor's best friend making areas desirable, being colorful sorts and all. Veritable canaries in a coal mine indicating impending disaster for poor neighborhoods. Trendy galleries and young hip couples soon moved in, colonizing the neighbourhood, disenfranchising starving artists and poor families alike; both priced out of the area.

He then drove through the old factory area, past the neighborhoods of dilapidated old mansions now serving as rooming houses for the most part.

The area's final blocks were dotted with boarded up houses and apartments where the homeless slept on porches, in backyards and sheds, or broke windows and moved in.

He swung the car up on to the expressway, heading north through the area of sixties urban renewal when the poor and working-class communities were razed without regard for the wishes of the residents, but in accord with the pious droning of social engineers unable to see or feel the vibrancy of life and culture. They saw only "eyesores", as if other people's poverty was a personal offense. They saw ugliness as defined by capitalism and consumption. Dirt and disrepair were the moral failings of lazy people; a racist view, also informed by class given that the area was largely made up of working-class African-American and Jewish neighborhoods.

Keith naturally loved the powerful photographs of life in the lost communities, taken by some great photographers. Although, like his own photos, none had the intimacy of even the most blurred and faded Polaroid snapped by a family member or friend, where an easy relationship between the photographer and subject was obvious.

Urban renewal had set off a frenzy of graft, grift, and kickbacks. Under the table money flowed as politicians from three levels of government doled out the tax dollars from working people to subsidize the wealthy. Of course, then as now, real estate and development are the primary businesses where the mob, bent politicians, and the wealthy collude for their mutual advantage.

After the bulldozing, the residents were dispersed and left to their own devices. Some had nowhere to go.

African-Americans were dispersed into the apartheid of the

projects, soon to be rife with crime and drugs. Their children, often unable to find work or afford an education, were then stacked like cord wood into the gulag, as pacified excess labor and voters. And harassed when leaving their zones.

The area Keith and Zach drove through was largely wasteland now, dotted with factories, strip malls, scrub land, and tenements. The highway was mainly a chute to funnel people to the suburbs. Real estate development and the laying of concrete had decimated nature, as always. Environmental laws are inimical to the greedy, so were eased just for them.

Beyond the city, in farm country, the pair went left at the "Kildonan turn off," informally named as such since Kildonan was a town of no renown about two hundred miles north. It spoke of what was notable long ago.

Following the ongoing, barked instructions from Zach, Keith drove two miles along the secondary highway that, according to the signs, led to a hamlet named Cordon.

They'd agreed on a plan. They passed Tennessee Butler's farm, with Zach slipping low in his seat, out of sight. Five hundred yards beyond it, Keith made a u-turn.

After again passing the farm, Zach popped up and his eyes began to search the bush to their right. "There, there," he said, waving in the direction of a small dirt road.

"Yeah, I see it," said Keith, who'd spotted the road a moment before and was already in the process of turning. Keith pulled the Civic as close to the right-side ditch as possible, leaving just enough room for a vehicle to pass by.

The two men climbed from the car and Zach stashed his cellphone under a rock so it couldn't be used to reveal his location. They walked back to the Cordon highway, crossed it, and dodged into the bush without being seen by any passing cars. They walked east and then turned south when after coming to wire fencing that surrounded the rectangular cow pasture situated between the house and the highway. A dirt drive lay on the other side of the pasture.

Keith deftly advanced through deciduous forest, checking his surroundings. Moving guerrilla war silently.

With his overstated stealth, Zach was more like a silent movie, buckskinned scout. One could almost hear the projector clacking and the Wurlitzer wheezing. All went well except for the proverbial snapped twig, "oops", stumble, "damn", or scratched face on a branch "shit".

Keith frowned each time, "shh!" Everyone's a critic.

They stopped several yards short of the front doors of the barn, just beyond the pasture, but still hidden from view.

Up an incline to their left was the white stucco farmhouse. None too ostentatious considering the wealth of the owner. Between the two structures was a grass and dirt clearing. A car and several motorcycles were parked there. Along the south perimeter of the clearing were three small out buildings.

From a front pocket, Keith removed the digital camera he always carried and held it in his hand.

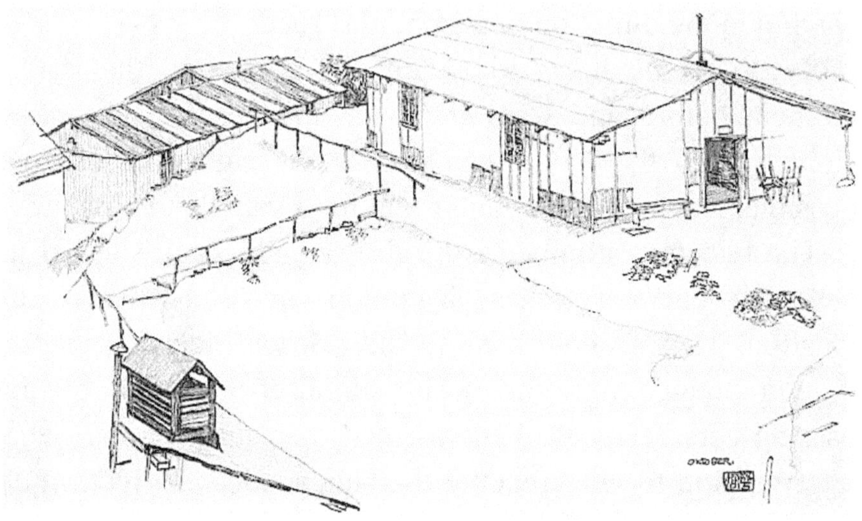

Only five minutes elapsed before the back door of the farm house opened and some men, laughing and in conversation, exited the house on to the long uncovered porch that traversed the length of the building.

Zach and Keith crouched lower but kept their eyes on the scene.

The first man out of the house, immediately on exiting, lit a cigarette and walked to the porch steps. Four other men followed him out, the last of which was Davey.

The man with the smoke in his hand walked down the stairs, accompanied by another. They started across the clearing, heading directly towards Zach and Keith near the barn doors, and were followed by a second pair of men similarly absorbed in talk.

Davey trailed along behind.

Keith brazenly, given the proximity of the men, snapped photos through the branches of the foliage. The conversations of both pairs of men were clearly audible as they passed, but of no consequence.

Davey was almost upon them when Keith became aware that Zach had tensed and re-positioned his feet, apparently ready to step out into the open. If that was his plan, it was canceled when a car suddenly appeared, moving up the dirt drive towards the house, trailed by a swirling cloud of dust.

It had caught Davey's attention too, causing him to stop and watch as the black vehicle drove to the house and followed the drive to the clearing behind it.

Davey turned and walked back to the car.

Tennessee Butler immediately emerged from the house, came rapidly down the porch stairs, and made his way to the driver's side door of the Mercedes convertible.

The driver, James Ross the Third, turned off the car engine and climbed out.

"What the fuck?" whispered Zach. "Was he part of the plan?" Throughout, he had elbowed, nudged, and tipped his head in silent communication to Keith telling him to record every new actor on the stage.

Keith scowled each time, neither needing a prompter, director or silent movie panel reading: "The Villains Arrive"! But he kept on with the camera, voraciously clicking away.

The three men began to converse. They were too far away from Zach and Keith – who was now filming the group – for the pair to hear what was being said. They stopped talking and turned when a passenger van, heading up the drive to the house, made its presence known.

James Ross immediately walked back to his car. He drove past the arriving van. Tennessee Butler returned to the house.

The van parked in front of the barn doors. As the driver climbed out, the two men who Zach and Keith had seen earlier, emerged from the barn with armloads of black plastic garbage bags and put them in the van.

Davey got into the van, started it up and maneuvered the vehicle past the house before swinging left on to the road leading to the highway.

Without needing to communicate with each other, Keith and Zach were running through the bush towards the highway, hoping to get to the Civic in time to follow the van.

"I'm coming back here with my camera," gasped Keith, "at night. I want to see what goes on in that barn."

"Under [Howard] Schultz [former Starbucks CEO], Starbucks touted its so-called 'social responsibility,' but it was for show. ... At the very same time, Starbucks kept some $1.9bn offshore to avoid paying US taxes – representing hundreds of millions in lost tax revenues that might otherwise have helped poor communities.

Social responsibility my macchiato. Starbucks spends millions each year lobbying the federal government, often seeking spending cuts along with the kind of tax breaks that continue to minimize Starbucks's tax bill."

– Robert Reich, 'Why Is The Media Showering Howard Schultz With Free Air Time?'

25.

It took Stella half a day to get to Kain, which is a satellite community of approximately 25,000 people just north of the city.

Blanche and Stella sat at one of the two cubicles along the

wall of a large room. Head high partitions on each side of the table provided some privacy from those in the next cubicles. A foot high plexiglass partition ran across the middle of the table.

Blanche was being held without charge, awaiting counsel's arrival from the city. But she'd had a brief conversation with a detective who had clarified to her that the painting she had in her possession when arrested was worth many millions of dollars and belonged to James Ross.

"I told the detective that I didn't steal anything," Blanche said. "I was delivering what I believed was a worthless painting to its owner."

"And that's all you said?"

"More or less. Once I understood that Zach and I had been set up I realized I should wait to speak to my lawyer before saying anything else."

The two women fell silent since they didn't know each other well. They executed the dance of the uncomfortable looking up, down, and around, avoiding eye contact.

"I'm glad you're holding up," Stella said eventually.

"I can't wait to get out of this place. Too many awful memories. I'm so pissed of at myself for getting involved in this. I knew there was something odd about the whole thing. I don't blame Zach. He's desperate for money. I could have said no to participating, but I didn't."

They fell into another awkward silence.

There was a huge wall clock behind them spitefully clicking out each minute, loud enough for everyone to know when their visiting time was up.

Blanche said, "Why hasn't Zach come forward?"

Stella explained where things stood, that during phone

calls Davey was denying any knowledge of the theft and was avoiding an in-person meeting with Zach. So Zach had gone to find him believing that Davey's corroboration was necessary to back up his own version of events.

Blanche said, "Zach is so naive. It's why they could dupe him into their scheme. Davey had to have been in on the plan. Angels don't hang out with mobsters. ... You think that maybe Zach was in on setting me up too?"

"No, no, of course not. He's very upset and knows he screwed up. He's going to come forward. I mean, he'll come forward soon."

"He's the only hope I have of the truth coming out."

Stella felt very sorry for Blanche and wished she could reach out and take her hand but had been told that physical contact was forbidden, hence the plexiglass wall between them.

"You'll tell me if he leaves the city won't you?" said Blanche.

"Of course, but he won't do that."

On the long bus ride, back to the condo, Stella gave a great deal of thought to the situation and possible courses of action.

She presumed that Tennessee Butler had intended to kidnap the painting for a ransom since it would be impossible to unload it, especially if, as she suspected, the thing was a forgery. She'd been an art major in college and knew something about the frequency of forgery. And that thought was the basis of a possible plan that began to take shape.

But it was a ludicrous idea ...

26.

Zach had reclined his car seat to be hidden from view.

Dexterously, Keith drove, filmed, and narrated at the same time.

"He's turning on to Fisher and now he's pulled over. Stopped in front of a variety store named Kim's."

"You're good at this; almost like you'd done it  before," said Zach with the guilelessness of an innocent.

"I'll just nip into this spot. That was a bit of luck." Keith's camera, that had been resting in the palm of his hand atop the dash, was now fluidly raised to his eye to better frame his subject. "I'm zooming in," he said. "Nice, I got Davey taking a black garbage bag into the store."

"Those bags could have cartons, packs, or bags of lose smokes in them, I think. He'll get some money and leave."

"The cops'll be interested in this," Keith said with relish.

Zach stole a quick glance up at his companion. They were on different pages. Zach had no interest in working with the police. He was only looking for something to bluff Davey with.

Davey exited Kim's, climbed into his van, and drove off.

Keith lay the camera on the dash while he put the car into drive. "He's leaving."

"I figured."

Keith began to follow. "We're going along Washington, shit, had to more or less run a red light." His face registered momentary panic.

"Don't get busted for god's sake. Don't do a Blanche."

Casting chastening eyes in Zach's direction, Keith said, "Okay. He's finally turning on to Water. Looks like he's going to Stella's bakery. Near enough, next door. I'll have to drive past. I don't see a spot to park. Shit."

"Here! Here! Give me your camera and stop the car."

Zach snatched the camera that was passed his way and scrambled from the car. As Keith drove away amid a charivari of blaring horns for his sudden stop, Zach crossed the sidewalk and ducked into the doorway of a store.

He filmed Davey taking a black bag from his van, glancing up and down the street at the traffic, and then slipping into the store. Zach kept the camera running after that, walking into the street, almost being run over, to capture an image of the storefront in a continuous take.

Keith would be thrilled later when he saw the video, saying that this would be the means to get back at the woman he'd encountered earlier who owned the store.

After he stopped filming, Zach walked up the street to reunite with Keith waiting in his car a long block away.

The two sat there until Davey had conducted his business and drove past them. Zach slid his bulk down on his car seat.

Minutes of silence passed before Keith said, "He's turning down a residential street. Didn't get the name. Now he's turning into a driveway. I'm gonna have to go past again. No wait. I'm gonna turn into this driveway. Stay low."

He drove the car into a driveway immediately across the

street from where Davey was parked, grabbed his camera and through the back window recorded Davey taking a plastic bag up to the side entrance of a house, and then, instead of returning to the van, entering the house behind the person who'd opened the door.

Keith kept filming as he climbed out of his car.

Zach's head emerged from behind the seat back, just enough to watch. His mask of the moment, casual fearlessness, slipped as he felt a surge of anxiety.

Keith cat walked the fifty feet or so to the back of Davey's van, opened one of the doors and removed a black bag. He scuttled back to his own car, still recording, and climbed in. He opened the mouth of the garbage bag and filmed inside.

"That's got him," said Keith, "we can head home now."

He backed his car out of the driveway and as they drove away Davey emerged from the side door of the house where he was parked. He remained in conversation with someone behind him, standing in the doorway.

"Ah you dumb fuck," muttered Keith, looking in his rear view mirror.

27.

The TV in Keith's livingroom was tuned to the news in case there was anything new regarding Blanche or the robbery. But the sound was turned low.

"I understand," replied Stella, after viewing the photos on Keith's camera, "but I don't even need to ask a lawyer to know that they'll be rejected in any court anywhere as proof that James Ross was in on the theft. But I think he was."

"I don't understand why anyone would conspire to steal their own painting," Keith said.

"Insurance money," said Zach.

"But that makes no sense," said Keith. "Ross could have sold the painting for a lot less hassle. Even if he got an insurance pay off for the painting, and still had the thing stashed away, it would be as good as gone since he couldn't display it or sell it. He may as well have sold it, since for all intents and purposes it's history."

"But," said Stella. "if the painting was hugely overvalued, which is easy enough to do, he might have gotten more money in insurance than he could ever sell the thing for, so a theft could be to his advantage, maybe by millions of dollars. And it would destroy the evidence if the painting is a forgery." After a pause, after debating whether to continue, she said, "But then there's another possibility. You steal your own painting and then ransom it to the insurance company. Say a painting is worth ten million. You sell it to the insurance company for two million. Since they don't know you're the crook you get your painting back plus the two million. The police don't like insurance companies doing this, but they do it anyway to save themselves a bunch of money, and because the police oppose it they conduct their business with the robbers on the sly which means they have a lot better chance of getting away with the scam."

"Sweet deal," said Zach, grudgingly.

"And even sweeter if the painting is over-valued."

"How do you know about this?" asked Keith.

"A lot of my friends work in the arts. It's not a big secret but proving it is difficult apparently."

Stella suddenly stiffened at the sight of James Ross the Third on the television news. "Wait! Wait!" she said, reaching for the TV remote to turn up the muted sound. There was a murmur of disapproval from the Greek chorus at the TV image. Stella raised the sound.

"I think, given the events of the last couple of days," James Ross was saying, "that in all likelihood the painting will be donated to an art gallery. It'll keep it safe, plus, with the publicity, there are many people anxious to see it."

The segment was near its end and it concluded with the on air reporter commenting on the noted largess and community spirit of the Ross family.

Their "generosity" was typical billionaire stuff. Pay no taxes then give a pittance to a charity that you deem is worthy rather than let the electorate decide what their community needs and have tax money spent on it. Take your bows and get the accolades for your grand beneficence.

Keith, Stella, and Zach sat silent, apparently absorbing the news. "You. Sneaky. Son-of-a-bitch," said Stella under her breath.

"What? What?" said Keith.

Stella, hit the mute button on the remote that she'd been squeezing in her hand. "Donating art is another scam for rich people like the Ross family. They get huge tax breaks from it and often pawn off work with suspect provenance. Actually, the theft of this painting will likely cause a buzz and the public will want to see it, which will make any gallery anxious to get it, so much so that they won't look at the thing too closely. A huge bonus if you're dealing with a fake."

"How do the owners get a painting falsely appraised?"

"Under the table money."

"And the galleries, who should know about this, don"t particularly care if something is falsely valued?"

"Not all, but enough. All monetary value is nonsense, just a market thing, but high prices drive up insurance costs so donating to a gallery unloads that."

"Crookedness and lying all round. Ripping off taxpayers. No wonder James Ross got into this business," said Zach.

"Well, back to the task at hand, I know what I'm going to do. I'm going to find Davey and force him to come with me to the cops to get Blanche free."

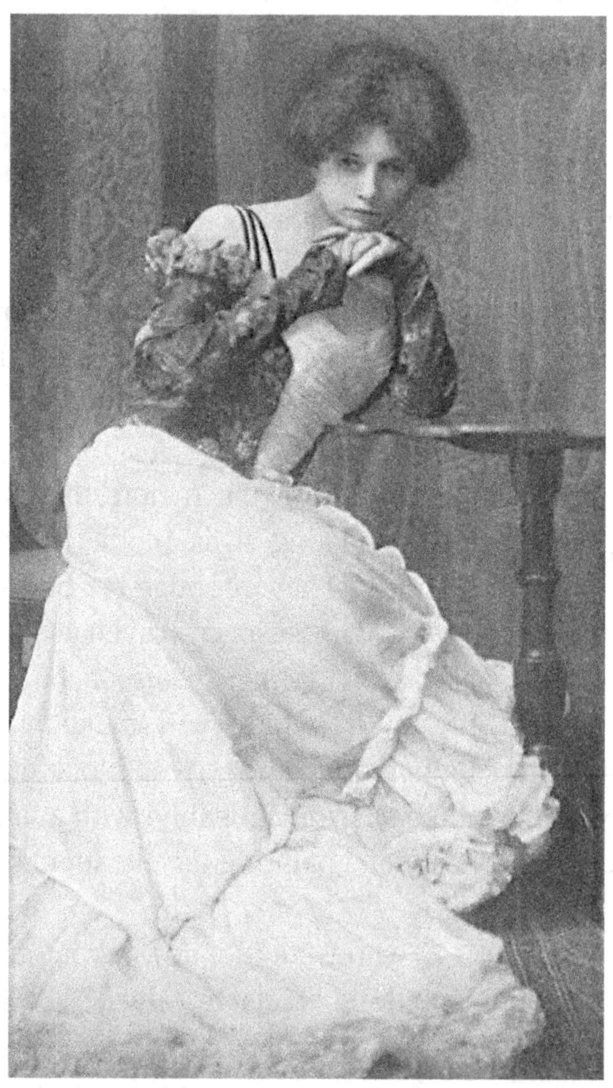

"I thought," said Keith, "that with the photos and the video of me stealing his cigarettes, not to mention the proof," he nodded towards the stolen black garbage bag on the floor, "that we could pressure Davey. But maybe the threat of a bit of jail time won't deter him."

"He could get some major jail time with his record," said Zach. "If it doesn't sway him then Blanche is screwed."

Stella said, "I've also been thinking about a plan to get her out. Plus, I think Davey will be all over himself to do anything to help."

And then she laid out her scheme. It took her all of thirty seconds.

"So what you're saying," said Zach slowly, "is that we make a copy of the painting and substitute it for the real thing. No valuable painting, no serious crime. And we use our photographs to pressure Davey into getting us into the Ross mansion to make the switch."

"Exactly."

"And he would go along with us why?"

"Because the photos and videos you have won't just get him jail time but will, at the very least, expose Tennessee Butler to scrutiny. The photos are pretty suggestive that he and the farm are involved in what's going on. The van exchange happened on his property after all. I doubt that Butler would be at all pleased at Davey for letting himself be followed and photographed. Plus, especially if Butler's involved, you'll be exposing a few of their clients, which would also piss off Butler. By switching the paintings Davey can put one over on Butler without him knowing who did it and make everything go away: jail time and Butler's anger. Once the switch is made then we can tip off the cops about the painting and get Blanche off. You can then turn yourself in Zach and say you were told it was a forgery so the police get someone to look at it."

"And who do we get to paint a credible forgery?" said Keith. "Do you know someone?"

"I do. Just the person. She's a street and graffiti artist, and if you look out your front window at the empty factory across the road, you'll see the location of her squat. The only thing is that now Ross sounds like he's going to unload the painting so we have to move fast."

"A donation is appraised at so-called fair-market value; and, while most types of charitable giving cannot exceed 20 percent of taxable income, for cultural properties the sky is the limit ... Of course, that opens up grand opportunities to scam the system."
– R.T. Nayler, Crass Struggle

love is a seditious act

PART 3

"The trees are typically rooted in cold, barren earth and silhouetted against a blank, unconsoling sky. Weak and frail, they almost invariably require supporting stakes and seldom carry more than a few leaves. 'One experiences an autumnal tree in summer most profoundly,' Schiele explained. 'This melancholy I want to paint.' Winter and autumn were for him the death forces against which the little trees vainly but nobly struggled."
– egon-schiele.com

28.

The second Schiele painting in the possession of the Ross family, produced around the same time as the first, was simply named 'Wildflowers'. Its provenance was even murkier than that of 'The Japanese Fire Tree', which at least had a customs document and gallery stamp. 'Wildflowers'

had found its way on to the Ross family dining room wall some time in the mid 1950s. James Ross II remembered being told that his grandmother had bought it shortly before she died, but that was all he knew.

The rumors that went around had it that the painting must have been smuggled into the country before WW2.

One version of the story was that it was likely stolen from a Jewish family by the Nazis. But there had never been any such claim made about a painting with its name, nor apparently was there any record of it to substantiate that or any other theory.

Another speculation was that it had been seized as "degenerate art" by the Nazi regime but then rescued from destruction by smuggling it out of the country in 1937. This would have been wise given that the seized art was burned in 1939 and 1942. Well, so they said. Some was sold and other pieces were kept by Nazi VIPs.

But Schiele wasn't one whose name was associated with the degenerate art purge. He was neither German nor a Jew, and he wasn't one of the artists whose work was involved in the 1937 Munich show of degenerate art. Plus, Adolph Hitler had applied to attend the Academy of Fine Arts Vienna, the same school that Schiele had attended – he was rejected – and it was the Fuhrer himself who had the final word on which art was degenerate.

In any case, after the death of Teresa, and despite Charles having placed their other works of art in the attic, 'Wildflowers' remained on the dining room wall.

It stayed there until the late seventies when it was moved to a guest room of the family mansion on the orders of James the First. Like his father, he didn't approve of foreigners or art, especially by a man whom he mistakenly assumed was German.

German industrial power had threatened his father's European investments but the krauts had thankfully been put in their place by the war and James didn't want to celebrate them in any way. Also, for some reason, he believed the painting was worthless, which was perhaps, an aesthetic judgment.

The painting was given to James the Third a short time after 'The Japanese Fire Tree' and the other paintings in the mansion's attic. By then III knew who Schiele was and also that he didn't want to pay the insurance on a second valuable painting. So he placed the painting in storage until the year before the theft of 'The Japanese Fire Tree'. After the painting was retrieved, he had it authenticated by a "Schiele expert", appraised, insured, and placed in his house.

"[Richard] Huelsenbeck and fellow Dada artists like Hannah Höch and George Grosz wanted to awaken people to the fact that 'Art, regarded from a serious point of view,' was 'a large-scale swindle.' This was especially true in Germany, where the most absurd idolatry of all sorts of divinities is beaten into the child, in order that the grown man and taxpayer should fall on his knees when, in the interest of the state or some smaller gang of thieves, he receives the order to worship some 'great spirit.'"
– Peter E. Gordon, The Politics of Art and Architecture at the Bauhaus 1919 – 1933

29.

Keith crossed the Cordon highway for the second time that day, scuttling low like he was landing on the beach at Normandy. It was 10 p.m.

Rain, wind driven on a westward angle, teemed down and thoroughly soaked his clothes. He took cover in the bush but the overhead branches, overloaded with raindrops, had long since been able to offer any shelter.

With the help of a penlight, Keith followed the trail that he and Zach had taken earlier in the day. In the distance he could make out the ghostly silhouette of the roof of Tennessee Butler's barn.

He stopped near the closed barn doors. Watched. Listened. Was that a dog? "Fuck."

Keith advanced along the side of the barn, not noticing the security camera mounted above him. A sleepy biker named Jeb who was watching the monitors, frustrated by the grey filter of the sleeting rain, his eyes strained, and working on his sixth beer of the night, didn't register the trespasser.

His flashlight now extinguished due to his proximity to the farm buildings, Keith twice stumbled over boulders of various sizes tossed there over the years as ground had been cleared for hay fields. Treacherous going. He went for a nosedive over an orphaned bastard rock. Another rock, and his stomach, soon connected with each other on the ground, leaving him momentarily winded and sapped of strength.

Unbeknownst to Keith, in the barn's underground bunker, several bikers were playing poker, sitting around a table in the tunnel just beyond the workbenches, shelves, and other fixtures of a meth lab. They slept in sleeping bags in the hay loft during the weeks of manufacture of meth or smokes but it was too early for bed.

The boys were low level gang members, mostly young, mostly dull, with the exception of the handsome one with long yellow locks who they called Lemony. He struggled with his conscience for making street drugs, wanted to live in China and translate the poetry of Li Bai. And he frequently railed against what he referred to as the "anglocentrism" in Ezra Pound's translations.

As was his wont, a biker named Kenny had been putting back more beers than anyone else. Nine by last count. It was a source of profound personal pride that he could not be drunk under the table by anyone.

"Goin' to take a leak," he announced suddenly, got up and headed toward the tunnel that exited behind the barn.

"You know it's pissing out there don't cha?" said one of his cronies.

"I like the fresh air," Kenny said over his shoulder.

"Fresh air? That's like saying you'll get fresh air at the bottom of a lake," said Lemony.

A chuckle went around, but Ken ignored it. He managed to avoid staggering, attempting to maintain the image he liked to project of invincibility in the face of alcohol, but once away from the scrutiny of the other bikers he allowed himself the pleasure of reeling a bit and bouncing lightly off the walls. At the end of the tunnel he climbed the ladder and with great difficulty raised the trapdoor above his head until it flopped over. It weighed in the area of sixty pounds because attached to it was two inches of cement, painted to look like dirt, and inserted into that was a variety of fake shrubbery to help it blend in with the surroundings.

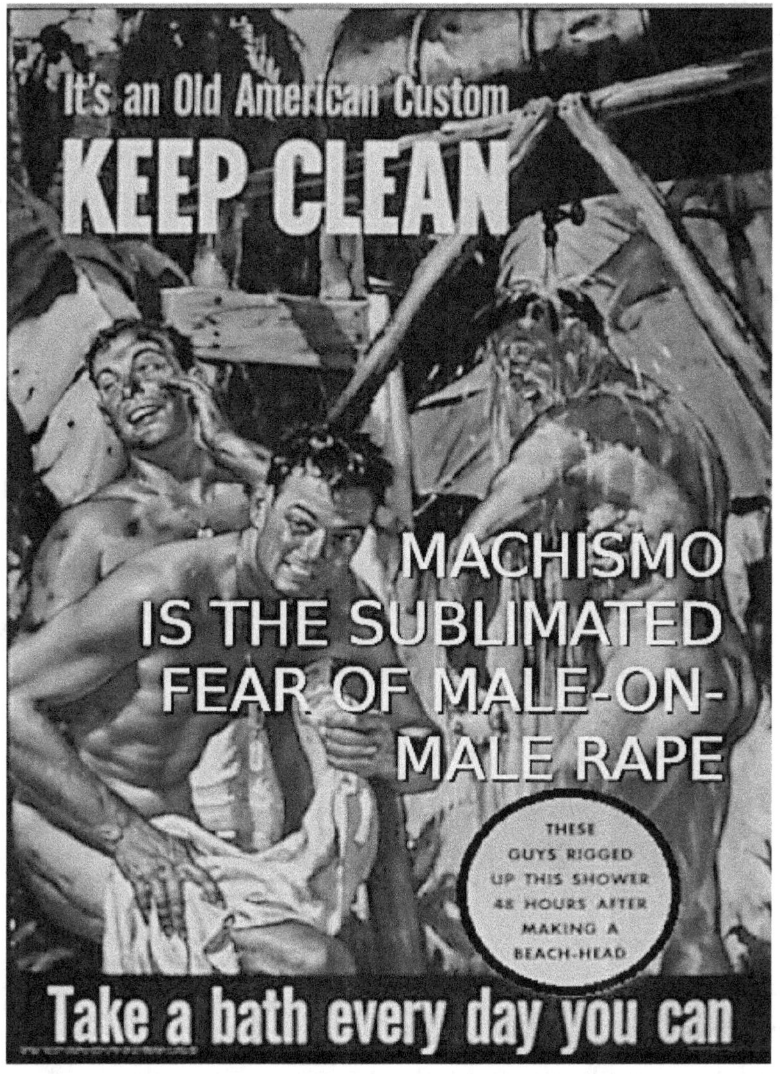

"Bitch!" he cursed at the door. "Fuckin' bitch," he said again on first being showered by the rain. It was ferociously pelting down now as if trying to wash clean his sorry soul, which would have been a thankless effort.

Kenny climbed out of the tunnel and tried to make a drunken run for the shelter of some trees but caught his toe on a small, half buried rock. He went over in drunken slow motion, arms at his side, like timber falling, his forehead colliding with a boulder that knocked him into a semi-conscious stupor, one step below his normal cognitive state. Blood began to ooze over his face.

In his short but eventful time outside, Kenny hadn't noticed the figure of Keith laying on the ground.

And Keith hadn't seen Ken either. But he heard the thud.

When Keith stood and saw Kenny he froze, then inched his way behind a nearby clump of trees while watching closely. There was just enough light coming from the open tunnel door for Keith to see that the man's face was soaked in blood. Was he dead? Should he check?

The sound of laughing voices in the tunnel startled him and the look of horror on his face indicated he was expecting to see someone emerge.

Spinning, and beginning to flee, he went face first into the first tree he came to, his ball cap flying backwards off his head. He reeled sideways, stunned, went down on one knee and then to his hands and knees. The bush swam and flashes of light dazzled his eyes.

Almost twenty minutes passed before Lemony set out on a search for the intrepid undersea adventurer named Kenny. Soon he made out his man struggling to stand up, bent at the waist, knees wobbling.

"You okay bro?" he said, taking an arm.

"Don't know Lemon Man." Kenny's mumbling was almost incoherent. His head made like a bobble head doll.

"What the fuck's all this blood on your face?"

"I fell, I think."

"Yeah, no shit." Lemony picked up the black ball cap

laying on the ground and put it on Kenny's head before slipping his hand under the guy's armpit to help him back to the tunnel.

Kenny, swiping with his free hand, knocked the offending hat to the ground. "Not my cap," he slurred but Lemony didn't pick up on the implication.

"You look like you fell down," said Carl when Kenny got back to the poker table. Master of the obvious.

"Yeah," agreed Fish. "You look like crap."

It was going on for midnight when a soggy and shivering Keith heard voices in the barn telling him the poker game in the bunker had broken up. It had been a miserable wait but he'd had to deal with much worse conditions during his military stint overseas.

As quietly as possible, Keith pried up the trap door. He turned on his camera, set it to film, and recorded the area outside the door to establish its location. He kept recording as he climbed down the stairs. At the bottom he switched on his pen light. Camera still rolling, Keith made his way along the tunnel. A poster taped to the wall, of a topless model dressed like a firefighter, shocked him into stopping. He'd translated the sight of a human form into the idea that here was a real person. Once past that misconception he gently edged his face around the turn of the tunnel. His penlight played over two steel tables in the middle of the room. A further inspection revealed a light switch. He took a chance and flicked it on. Looking about, he had a pretty fair idea that this was a meth lab but he needed to check with Zach. Zach would know.

Keith videotaped everything in the room. Satisfied that he'd gotten a continuous take, long enough to prove that the lab was beneath Butler's barn, Keith stopped the video function and began to take some snaps.

Fifteen minutes later, Keith was back in his car driving towards the Kildonan turn off.

The next morning, at 9:15 a.m. Keith phoned Crime Stoppers to report the meth lab at the Butler farm and explain how to find its entrance.

He made his call from the bush near the farm. His car was hidden from view on the opposite side of the highway.

Keith walked on to the barn and took up his watch.

At 10:22 a.m. a police car drove up to the farm and pulled into the clearing in front of the barn. Tennessee Butler emerged from the house as two officers climbed from the car. The three of them shook hands. They chatted for a couple of minutes before the men climbed back into their car and left. Tennessee stood and watched them go then turned and stared thoughtfully at the barn.

On the drive leading from the farmhouse to the road, the departing car passed a black sedan.

Butler turned and noted the second vehicle. He waited.

Keith had been ferociously snapping photographs the whole time and was confident he'd gotten at least one clear image of the license plate of the departing car, and now that of the second vehicle as it pulled up beside Tennessee Butler.

The chief of police climbed out.

Keith snapped another shot and under his breath said. "So no investigation, just a tip off to Tennessee and a visit. Bastard." Undoubtedly, he decided later, this would be followed by a claim back at the station that the farm had been searched and the call about the meth lab had been a hoax.

The chief and Butler were photographed laughing together.

After the chief left, Butler disappeared out of sight around the opposite side of the barn. Apparently it had occurred to Butler that there were only two ways that anyone could have known about the entrance to the meth lab. Either they were spying or one of the people at the farm was a rat.

When Keith heard the German Shepherd's bark he was up and running through the bush. Whether the dog had seen him or smelled him, Keith didn't know, but by the time he got to the highway the dog was right behind him.

Keith stopped and turned. The dog stopped as well. Keith carefully bent low and picked up a two foot long piece of branch for protection. It was hefty, a couple of inches across. He held it in front of him as he backed up, all the while making soothing comments. The dog growled and snarled, making short lunges as if it were about to attack.

In that manner, Keith and the dog crossed the highway and began down the road towards his car. It suddenly occurred to Keith that time was of the essence, plus he was fed up. His voice became angry. "Get the fuck outta here!" he said to the dog and strode towards him.

The dog was no fool. He knew cruelty and he knew to escape it. Presumably having identified Keith as just one more violent prick, the dog stopped snarling, turned, and ran back towards the farm.

"When students rioted in Chicago in 1968 their demands included the abolition of money and the acknowledgment that every human being is an artist."
– Modris Eksteins, Solar Dance: Van Gogh, Forgery, and the Eclipse of Certainty

"Every form of authority – family, state, and religion in particular – attempts to control who we love and hate based on gender, colour, religion, class, ability, ethnicity, or sexual preference. The reasons for this include political and financial aims, and to enhance the institution's power.
But love is a river that flows where nature wills it to go so these attempts to direct its course with hate, prejudice, violence, and authoritarianism are like so many useless boulders placed in the rapids. Love swirls and eddies, over and around them, eventually grinding them down to nothing.
Love is a seditious act and this must be so."
– Ted Fox, Review of Beautiful In My Worn Clothes

30.

Those present at the meeting in Stella's bakery – besides Stella of course – were Zach, Belle, Donal McGraith, Keith, and Stella's friend Kalie, who owned a mural printing business in the storefront next door. There was no secret cabal, word had spread among friends knowing no one would side with the Ross family and turn Zach in.

Belle looked at Zach's photograph of *The Japanese Fire Tree* and the dimensions. She said that she liked the plan and could do the forgery, however she needed to actually be able to examine the original, including the back. She wanted to see if there were gallery stamps or other indicators of provenance. Another of her concerns was to see if the painted area extended around the stretcher frame or just to the edge of the canvas. She felt an appraiser would have examined every inch of it carefully and taken photos. The forgery had to look like the painting in every respect or else it would be apparent on examination that a switch had been made, and that wouldn't help Blanche. Belle promised that if she did the copy she would do something to make it clear the painting was a forgery, but not something so obvious as to be immediately evident, just something that an appraiser might have missed.

Her response caused quite a bit of consternation but the consensus was that Davey would just have to be made to agree to facilitate two visits rather than one.

Keith spent considerable time studying Belle, the woman in the squat who was ripe for saving. Or so he'd thought. He wasn't sure any more. He spoke up though, to tell his tale of the previous morning and what he'd witnessed at Butler's farm which suggested that the police had no interest in investigating Butler's activities.

Donal said, "Have you managed to contact Davey by phone to try to get his co-operation or set up a meeting?"

"No, his cell is no longer in service. I was just thinking that I should leave a message on the landline he called me from. I think it's Butler's."

Donal said, "Since Butler might hear any messages you obviously can't threaten to expose Butler's connection to Davey's black market cigarette business, or tell him you photographed his customers. Keeping that information from

Butler in exchange for Davey's help is your bargaining chip."

"Yeah, good point I guess," said Zach with an artisanal frown.

"You have to make the threat of exposure face to face."

"Agreed. But I've been watching his place and he hasn't come home yet."

"Perhaps you could compel him to call you."

"How?" asked Keith, with an unintended blank look.

Donal said, "You could post some of the photos of the meth lab and the chief of police on line. Even print them up and paste them to some buildings downtown. Block out the faces and any tell tale signs that the thing is located below

Butler's barn. That way Davey will be pressured by Butler and the police chief to contact you to get you to shut up. Sign the posters in some way so that he knows they're being posted by you. Then, when you meet him, you can show him the cigarette photos. I know that the law doesn't apply to him and Butler, and that if publicly exposed they'll just shut down the meth lab, but by posting the photos you're showing them that you can reach people directly and destroy reputations."

"And I can get some people to paste them up," said Belle. "The posters could be enlargements of photos of the meth lab with a caption like: "Can you guess the location of this meth lab?"

There were murmurs of approval. It was generally agreed that Butler might panic knowing about the photos and that it would hurt his business if the location of the meth lab ever came out, putting the police under pressure to prosecute him.

Someone suggested that after the painting was switched that the postering could resume and the video put up online so that the meth lab would be closed down.

The whys and wherefores of making posters came up. That generated some intense interest after Donal challenged some of the group's assumptions about the need for skilled artists and for hard to remove posters. He gave at least a dozen examples of impermanent, creative, civil disobedience. Some of these generated laughs and others inspired new and copycat ideas. Donal was Socrates to the group, challenging everything as a rule, and the sage for several.

And just like that, the aim came to be something more than freeing Blanche. It also became about creative activism to expose the criminal gang running the city and to challenge the power of the Ross family by using humor and humiliation.

31.

That night, an amateurish poster using three of Keith's photos was pasted up all over downtown. One photo showed the trap door to the lab, another the lab itself, and the third was a photograph of Tennessee Butler and the out of uniform chief of police having a discussion at Butler's farm, with their faces and the chief's license plate blacked out.

The caption read: "Can you guess whose barn this meth lab sits under and why the police don't close it down?" At the bottom, in small letters, it read. "Call me." And it was signed, "The Irishman." It was a subtle way of telling Davey to call Zach. The latter was confident Davey would understand since Davey sometimes called him, "The Irishman".

There was no phone response from Davey the next morning. Zach, the city's most notorious "person of interest", with furrowed forehead and much muttering, paced his personal lion's cage, making frequent forays to the apartment's front window to look over at Davey's place.

"I've been thinking," Keith said after supper, "that it won't be safe to show up for a meeting with Davey if he calls you to set one up. He can set it in an out of the way place and get some of Butler's biker friends to show up when you get there."

"So what am I going to do then?" said Zach.

"I'd say, just what you're doing now. You watch the window. When Davey calls you insist the meeting be at his place. Presumably he'll show up before the meeting starts and then we can ambush him. Or, if we're lucky, he just decides to go home and when we see the lights on in his place we can push our way in."

32.

The following morning the city awoke to find that a few dozen image blow-ups of various sizes had been pasted around the downtown on building walls, bus shelters, and utility boxes.

The photographs were all homemade family photos. Some were blurry and most poorly framed. They appeared to be from the nineteen-fifties and sixties. Some, because they didn't have enough pixels for such an enlargement, required distance and angle to make them discernible.

They were all beautiful and evocative images of people who had lived in the area and shaped it. The images gave them a tangible presence, as if the city had a living memory of its past. The faces reflected every variant of skin color and background.

The City Manager was outraged. "You can't do something like this without a permit," he was quoted as saying by the local Ross media. "This is vandalism pure and simple. It's now a serious police matter."

The Tribune added an outraged editorial along the same lines. It was an aesthetic issue, they said, declining to comment on the beauty of the paid advertising found on every surface downtown. Presumably, since advertisements were bought and paid for, they were aesthetically pleasing. And since when was public access free?

Some guessed that their outrage was because the posters seemed to presume that the people, rather than the Ross family, owned the city.

All of the posters on city property were torn down that same day. Many on private buildings and utility boxes remained. They were left to disintegrate over time, subject to the elements and vandalism.

33.

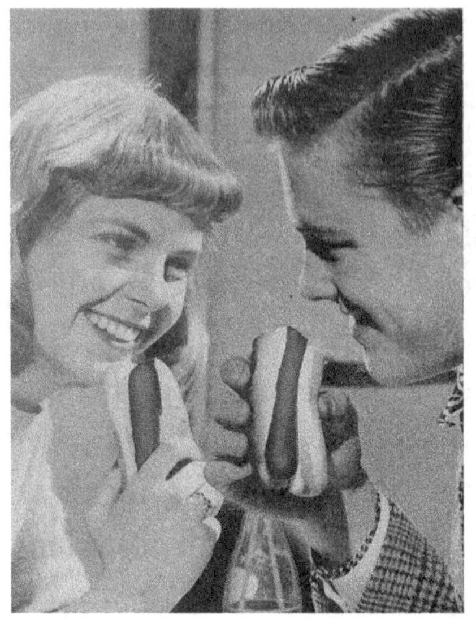

The next morning revealed that overnight someone had followed The Tribune delivery truck while making its rounds downtown and stocking up the twenty or so newspaper boxes there.

The culprit(s?) put in enough change to open each box, dumped a large amount of Crazy Glue around the edge of the doors, and sealed the boxes shut. They then pasted an 8.5" x 11" photo-copied sheet to the plastic window on the box door.

The message on the sheet of paper read:

```
In a way, the world-view of the Party imposed
itself most successfully on people incapable of
understanding it. They could be made to accept the
most flagrant violations of reality, because they
never fully grasped the enormity of what was
demanded of them, and were not sufficiently
interested in public events to notice what was
happening. By lack of understanding they remained
sane. They simply swallowed everything, and what
they swallowed did them no harm, because it left no
residue behind, just as a grain of corn will pass
undigested through the body of a bird.
—George Orwell, 1984
```

This was of course recognized as an affront by those at The Tribune, but they weren't overly worried about the financial impact, since it was minimal. At a management meeting it was decided that the act had been a conspiracy committed by "radical socialist Democrats" at the urging of some nebulous group of "leaders".

They decided to smother the event rather than "give it air". They did, however, briefly mention it in an editorial the next day where they denounced "the scourge of socialist dupes". And they quoted from White House aide (and alleged member of Vitézi Rend, a Nazi-linked group) Sebastian Gorka's recent speech from the CPAC that had been covered as extensively as The Tribune ever covered anything, with a few crazy quotes and lots of photographs. Gorka had claimed that socialists wanted to take away American's pick-up trucks and hamburgers. "This is what Stalin dreamt (sic) about but never achieved". God Bless America and red meat.

"For there to be any space for the aesthetic there must be mistakes, incompleteness, impermanence. The masterpiece is sealed up with a bow, it is vapid, vacant, closed. Any personally valuable aesthetic experience must either be failure or teetering on the edge of failure. Art should be an attempt to live in a different world and because that world does not exist we can only fail. The artist documents her failure. The failed attempt to make something beautiful is an indication of a possible life we know can exist.

When a painting by Picasso sells for fifty million dollars, it is pure anti-art. Any joy in that art was sucked out. The money stands for nothing, it cares about no one; it flows while we all burn up and waste away. The painting is no longer emblematic of human striving, but an empty symbol of greed."

– Donal McGraith, Leaving No Mark: A Prolegomena To An Evanescent Art

he could walk down your street
and girls could not resist to stare
Pablo Picasso was never called an asshole
– Jonathan Richman (Modern Lovers), lyrics, 'Pablo Picasso'
(variously covered by David Bowie, John Cale, and Iggy Pop)

34.

My discovery that certain unknown persons had been defacing library art books happened by accident. I was researching a topic in one such book and was struck by some odd highlighting. Here's a representation of my first find.

the "student of Pissaro" a major influence on modernism, especially via the 'genius' (keeping in mind the attempt to abolish it as a descriptor notion in post-modernism) Pablo

It suddenly occurred to me that this was the title of Nikita Sunburn's tome *Piss on Modernism, Shit on Post-Modernism*. I went through a number of the library's art books and they were all marked up and defaced with slogans and quotes from Sunburn and his "layabout" [Dick Blick, The Tribune] friends in the seventies group, F-Art. They were especially known for disrupting cultural events while clad in matching white outfits and lots of make-up. It seemed that the war on art was still on.

The F-Art Manifesto

What is F-Art?

What does it stand for?

F-Art stands for no one. F-Art-ists remain seated during the national anthem. Will you all rise? F-Art says, NO.

F-Art is Fake Art. All art is fake. The F-Art group accepts this as wholly true. There is no originality. F-Art rejects the jargon of authenticity and its petty kneeling subservient theology. Picasso is not god or Pan. All Picassos are fake.

F-Art is Free Art. Art without a price tag. F-Art rejects the art market as money laundering for scoundrels. Every piece of 'art' in the museum has blood on it. It is all stolen. It is all fake.

F-Art rejects Personal Style Art. Style is the straight jacket for the mad artist. The artist is insane because once she has a style she is ever condemned to repeat the same damn thing. We will do whatever we want whenever we want. We refuse to make art. We refuse to be arty. We refuse to be creative. We refuse to be dull.

F-Art is Flatulent Art. We recognize the anality of art. We acknowledge that art is playing with shit. We recognize that art stinks. Like flatulence, art smells sickly sweet to the flatulator but disgusting to others. We reserve the right to disgust you.

F-Art is Failed Art. We reserve the right to remain art failures. We reject the idea that we are geniuses because our art sells. Shit sells. Our failed art is not for sale, we will not be bought. Our art is our own free activity and you cannot have it. We revel in our failure to make good art. If our art is not good we must be doing something right.

F-Art means Fuck Art. Yes, Fuck Art! It's all so boring and it's all so over. What is the difference between Damien Hirst and Ronald McDonald (sic)? Over 1 million paintings sold here. Thomas Kinkade and Damien Hirst are the same person. Why buy it if you can do it yourself?

F-Art is Fine Art. Artists should be fined for polluting. Stop already! Since art historians, art critics, hipper-than-thou art galleries, and art museums are basically in the business of money laundering for scoundrels who pollute, steal and impoverish, all art should be taxed. Tax art to death. Art history is merely advertising for Christie's. No one buys these monstrous books.

35.

One evening, sometime after midnight, a figure in black pants and hoodie emerged from an office in the city's highest downtown tower. CCTV cameras didn't pick up the person until they were in the stairwell. It was impossible to tell from the recording whether the culprit was a man or a woman. In any case, the person climbed the last few flights of stairs and jimmied the door leading on to the roof. There was no alarm on the door. In their left hand they held a large stack of paper. On each was printed an essay entitled, "The United States of Impotence".

There was a high wind that night. The person left the papers on a corner of the rooftop and used the wind to distribute their flyer (pun intended). The person managed to get out of the building without being apprehended. This distribution method was soon adopted for a variety of work.

The United States of Impotence

One recent example of the increasing impotence of many white American men was the election of Donald Trump to the presidency. Remember when someone admitting to sexually assaulting women would have excluded them from the presidency? No more.

Many men voted for Donald Trump, and many claim to have a certain strength (calling others "snowflakes"), truly believing that they stand up for their country, for their daughters and sons, and for the children of others. But they don't. Not when they elect a man who is a bully, who brags about sexually assaulting women, and who actively:

• destroys women's and all other rights that fundamentalists dislike, one result has been to make the world far more dangerous for women, immigrants, minorities, and LGBTQ people

• who engages in hate speech which is largely responsible for the huge increase in hate crimes

• who guts a UN resolution seeking an end to rape as a weapon of war, and who sides with male rapists at colleges over victims

• who, in an effort to court votes, champions a "Christian" faction which aims to install a theocracy based on male supremacy, controlling the bodies of women no matter how many die as a result (a hypocritical group which, in turn, supports a political party which has killed millions of women and children in the last few decades alone)

• who supports the starvation of the children of Yemen, seeks to murder Iranian and Venezuelan children through economic sanctions and war, supports the killing of Palestinian children, locks children in cages, and turns a blind eye to poverty and to those living on the streets

• who, because his only value is money, is actively increasing the destruction of the earth, the birthright of our children and grand-children, and whose policies will contribute to the deaths of millions if not billions as the earth is rendered uninhabitable

• who is doing everything in his power to strip healthcare from millions of American children and working people

• who is leading the world closer and closer to nuclear annihilation, abandoning treaties and targeting China

What kind of gutless, so-called men would support this president, a man who admires and supports the new incarnation of fascism? Who betrays our ancestors who fought and died opposing fascism and white supremacy. A man who threatens violence against his critics.

The answer is white, impotent men. Men who:

• quiver in their boots at the thought of Muslims, people of color and gay people, and are filled with loathing as a result of their cowardice

• who arm themselves to the teeth and shoot first, so terrified are they of others and convinced of their own weakness

• whose idea of warfare is (from a safe spot) to send out drones that slaughter children and other civilians

• who recognize that "Make America Great Again" is code for restoring white, male privilege to the impotent

• who can no longer support their families on their wages or buy them the things they want because of political policies that have shifted wealth to the very wealthy, and who are such mindless sheep as to be convinced that leaving the wealthy in charge (i.e. oligarchy / daddy figures) will change this and restore their personal self-esteem

• who often participate in the anonymous bullying of women and people of color who speak up (attempts to control come from fear)

• who live in fantasy worlds of football heroes and super-hero movies in a perpetual adolescence, and suck up revisionist myths of cowboys as rugged, individualist entrepreneurs

• who stand up, salute, and regurgitate whatever bilge has been pumped into them to justify slaughtering millions around the world for America's wealthy

• who have been indoctrinated into fear, such as that of the dreaded boogeyman of socialism, which roughly translates as any effort to spend their tax dollars on them or the needy rather than the wealthy, and has allowed the wealthy to define this as freedom

Yes, we are all fundamentally impotent to a great extent in this modern world where we rely on commodities and experts. Remember when people could live self-sufficiently, build their own homes, grow their own food, and make their own clothing and entertainment? Those days are lost and maybe gone forever.

Yes, there are many white women who also support Trump. Who feel the loss of their white privilege and who think that Trump's policies can give them back the income they have lost and turn their husbands into men rather than the sniveling cowards they've become. But white, male Trump voters are in a class of impotence, crawling cowardice, and hypocrisy all their own.

"Art [geijutsu] is not a special thing. Anyone can do it. Making art does not have to be so unusual. What I mean is that middle-aged men and housewives, your neighbours, can also do it. Being an artist is not so unusual. If everybody were to become an artist, what we call 'Art' would disappear. I think it would be fine if this were to happen and [what I have envisioned] becomes a reality."
– Yoko Ono (1964), as cited in 'Some Young People – From Non Fiction Theater: Transcript of a Documentary Film directed by Nagano Chiaki' (found in Art, anti-art, non-art: experimentations in the public sphere in postwar Japan, 1950-1970 / edited by Charles Merewether with Rika Iezumi Hiro)

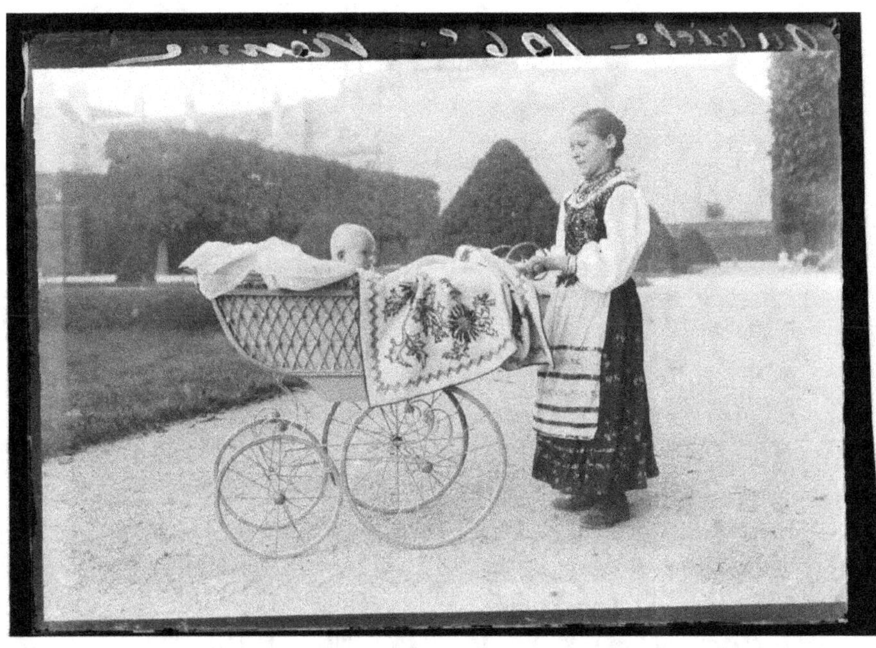

The scene occurs at an art gallery. Adam and Allison address a young artist:

Allison Schrager "Not only is the fine art world manipulated financially, it's also extremely exclusive. Only a small share of artists are allowed to succeed and only their work is considered valuable." ...

Adam Conover "And that means this small group of ultra wealthy investors ends up defining what fine art is."

– Adam Ruins Everything, How the Fine Art Market is a Scam, truTV

https://www.youtube.com/watch?v=Dw5kme5Q_Yo

36.

As the flyer on impotence was raining down on the city, someone was pasting up the first of their notorious "America is the greatest country on earth" posters. Each featured an illustration with a caption and then a list of examples. They included these lines.

On unfair taxation[1]:

> ### Another "America is the greatest country on earth" fun fact:
>
> - In 2018 Amazon paid no U.S. tax on a profit of $11 billion and they received a $129 million tax rebate.

On press freedom and press ownership:

> ### Another "America is the greatest country on earth" fun fact:
>
> - In its 2019 rankings, Reporters Without Borders ranked the U.S. 48th in the world for Press Freedom.

Posters covered many aspects of American life, including healthcare, gun deaths, civilians killed by police, education, civil rights, suicides, the state of American democracy, and incarceration levels of men of color. Collectively, they showed the disparity between what capitalist and political dogma said about the U.S. compared to the reality.

---

1   On the subject of tax breaks for corporations (for job creation): Norman Decarie has noted in his blog that corporations do not make money from creating good jobs but by cutting them and by paying as little as possible.

Another "America is the greatest country on earth" fun fact:

America is unrivaled in its ability to kill children in a single day

Hiroshima atomic bomb
Aug. 6, 1945
est. 52,000 child deaths

Tokyo bombings
Mar. 9, 1945
est. 35,000 child deaths

Nagasaki atomic bomb
Aug. 9, 1945
est. 26,250 child deaths

The posters were either the output of a diverse group or one or two very prolific activists because over the next several nights other posters also appeared attacking the Ross family; just as if no frightening line was being crossed by this. They were pasted up on telephone poles and the doors and sides of buildings. The posters were scanned and sent out as tweets, Facebook posts, blog entries, and in other forms. Some caught on and were widely circulated.

Can you spot the difference?

Westboro Baptist Church nut job sign

upstanding American patriot sign

Trick question! There is no difference.

One series, "Ecological Reality," exposed some of the effects of the Ross family's forest and mill operations; companies that benefited from public lands. The accompanying images ranged from the pleasant – like the beautiful bird on the poster providing stats about the millions of bird deaths caused by clear-cutting – to an obscene graphic showing the toxic effluent from the Ross pulp and paper mill. These posters were attached to trees, using biodegradable tape, in parks, and along running and bike paths.

Another series was dubbed "The Myth of the Self-Made Man". Each poster revealed a way in which the public was subsidizing the Ross family. One showed a Ross business that had been given a contract to provide products to the government, without tendering the contract. Another detailed how local taxes had been waived for an oil refinery on the waterfront; a tax savings of millions of dollars per year (and noting that the Ross family used off-shore accounts to avoid paying taxes).

Yet another series was an attack on the art gallery's sponsors. These posters were taped up – on the inside – of the huge front window of an alternative gallery. They detailed a bevy of shady operators and sleazy exploiters of people and the environment, here and around the world, and they especially focused on the Ross family. Each poster revealed a particularly vile activity by the sponsor; some exposing that the funds donated were blood money.

There didn't seem to be any central organization to the activist work being done. The only commonality appeared to be the rejection of authority since threats by politicians and police to jail the street artists only led to an explosion of more acts. Even kids and seniors got in on the fun. A nursing home resident, for one, did an enormous mural, exposing the hate behind the phrase "God is on our side" which justifies all sorts of depravity against others, and pasted it up on one wall of her room. Photos of it circulated widely.

The city was also being plastered with graffiti – my favorites being those that drew attention to the demise of ontology in our post-truth world. Slogans like "Reality is dead, deal with it", "All news is fake", "This is not a wall", and "True is false and false is true", were everywhere.

Of course the propaganda purveyors and watchdogs at The Tribune and Ross Media TV and radio stations, were sent into paroxysms of paranoia and hate, dubbing the criticisms "fake news", while imagining communists under every bed and behind every rock with their beady eyes on overthrowing "our perfect empire" (Dack Blinks, The Tribune).

The call went out for more authoritarian measures. More police to protect the critical vacuum. The official thought police were soon swarming the downtown area after dark.

As well, bikers drove along city streets and gangs of three or four men walked with them to extend the police gaze. The impotent always support tyranny. The police officially frowned on the vigilantes but it soon became apparent that where the gangs were the police weren't, and vice versa.

The Tribune frowned on the "breakdown of law and order" but saw the gangs as "freedom fighters" (Dirk Flicks, The Tribune).

Avoiding these physical risks led to more than a dozen new blog and website start ups over the next few weeks featuring analysis, commentary, and satiric content. Flyers rained all over the city. They were left on tops of buses, bridges, and buildings of all heights. Catching posters became a game, like snagging beads during Mardi Gras. Billboards were détourned, and somehow, murals showed up on building walls and streets. Perhaps as many as fifty videos were posted online. There was analysis, documentary, appropriation of ads and imagery combined with critical commentary, or putting new words into old mouths.

ALL

NEWS

IS

FAKE

Both political parties were critical of the activists. "So look what we have now," bewailed a Democrat running for state senate. "Everyone's expressing their 'creativity'." His voice dripping with disdain. "This is no way to accomplish change. There are proper channels for it. Vote for me and give me your trust and I will speak for you."

It surprised me when I first saw work that mentioned Donald Trump. Even the attacks on American dogma were just that and not about individual politicians. Plus Trump is the most boring man in the country. A liar without helpful ideas or accomplishments. A racist, xenophobic, sexist, coward and clown. Only with the end of the real could Donald Trump have become president. He is a fake billionaire, living a life of opulence masking the fact that he is a fake successful businessman. A fake real estate mogul who plants his name on buildings he doesn't own. A false front. And a front man. A fake president who wasn't even elected.

If anything, the majority of the work going on in the streets questioned the possibility of substantive change about issues like healthcare coming from either of the main political parties. As well, the subversion devoted to reclaiming the city, and exposing the practices of the Ross businesses and their criminal practices, didn't endorse anyone.

Eventually I saw that the work about Trump was also exposé and it was done because of the unique danger that he posed to America and the world.

Trump was putting the entire planet in grave danger of environmental destruction and nuclear war. He stood for unfettered capitalism, hate, and imperialism. Domestically, he was mounting an attack on human rights and liberal democracy, and he aspired to be a fascist ruler.

An entertaining dalliance was the blog titled *Trump Lists*.

One list was an extensive elaboration of the ways in which the president was still a spoiled, bratty child. The junk food diet, temper tantrums, short attention span, short briefing notes with pictures, know-it-all attitude, bullying, name calling, need to be the center of attention, feeling persecuted, constant bragging, continual lying, etc, etc.

This was part of a list done in the form of Trump's third grade report card showing his astonishing ignorance, compelling in a watching-a-train-wreck kind of way, especially horrifying in that this was an individual with colossal power to effect the future of the globe and mankind but who willingly remained ignorant of even basic facts. With "teacher comments" that mentioned things like Trump's invention of an African country (maybe it's a small country like "Whales"), having no knowledge of global warming, thinking the moon is part of Mars, and never having heard of Frederick Douglass, he was, not surprisingly, given an F in every subject.

Another list included many of the ways in which the presidency paralleled a mafia organization. Ma familia. Loyalty and silence were the order of the day in the White House as they are in any mob. A number of the items involved the many people who'd been indicted, jailed, or forced to resign in scandal that were part of Trump's administration. Entries also included various laws that had been changed that made criminal activity easier to get away with. And, of course, the allegations regarding family and associate ties to the Russian mafia were plentiful as well as the instances of the president's family personally profiting by their political power, etc, etc.

I hoped that the blog writer might do a similar list concerning our state and city mobs with their bought politicians, political favors, graft, and tax breaks.

But this is not to suggest that the city was not a subject of the street art and other work. Far from it.

One such effort occurred on a Monday evening. Stella and Kalie left the bar at midnight, went back to Kalie's, and made love. They slept till 2:00 a.m., woke up, made love again till the last possible moment, around 3:15 a.m., then got up and headed out.

What happened next might be seen as a continuance of their exuberant expressions of love.

For the following hour Stella used her cupped hands to boost the wee Kalie so she could decorate street signs with peel and stick bumper stickers that had been printed by a friend the previous night in the print shop that she owned.

Each bumper sticker was made to look like the municipal road signs that identified street names, but instead of names of men, they featured the names of women, famous and not, who'd lived in the area.

Some Jefferson Street signs were stickered over with Elizabeth Brown Street signs, named for a local suffragette leader. And some Washington Avenue signs were covered over by Ruby Speck Avenue signs, claiming the street on behalf of a civil rights leader and peace activist who'd been murdered by the local police in 1968.

A map would soon be distributed, on a flyer, granting new names to all of the downtown streets. (On the flip side were photos.) Some streets were named for women, and others seemed to be editorials. For example, the financial center was on a street re-named Greed Street and the largest mall was on Useless Crap Way.

The shop that did the stickers was thereafter inundated with business. Stickers placed on the back of bus seats urged people to call in sick for work. Bumper stickers reading "Ministry of Truth" were applied to Tribune boxes, and "I'm a polluting asshole" to large personal vehicle bumpers.

The street where Kalie and Stella were living at the time was re-named "Love Street".

Another "America is the greatest country on earth" fun fact:

America Is Not A Democracy

Super PACs. *Money buys elections. An unlimited amount of money can be donated and spent on individual campaigns and donor identity can be masked.*

Gerrymandering. *The conservative dominated Supreme Court has confirmed that electoral boundaries can be redrawn to ensure that (usually) Republican candidates will be elected in spite of losing the popular vote.*

The Senate *gives equal seats to all states. A generally conservative state with less than a million people can erase the voices of a liberal state with 40 million people.*

The Electoral College *elects the president and their choice may not reflect the popular vote. A few swing states with a small percentage of the population effectively picks the president.*

*Not to mention **Russian election interference** and **voter registration laws** that disenfranchise voters.*

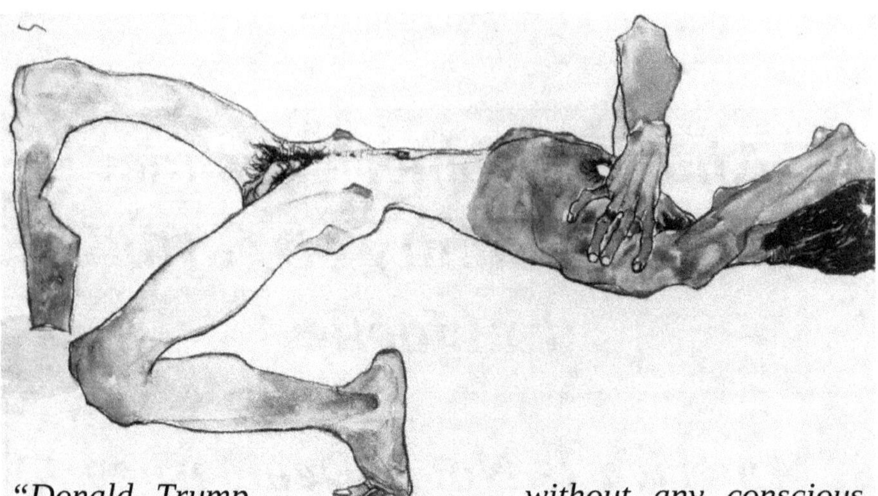

"Donald Trump, without any conscious understanding of the meaning of what he says or his own actions, is the embodiment of a kind of surrealist conundrum: This Is Not A President, not because he is incompetent or corrupt but because there is no ideology at all. It's always been about counterfactuals. There is no guile because there is no business. There is no product. There is only a brand. Trump sells a pure idea: money for nothing. Somehow Trump can sell the idea of failure as success. You make some declaration, let there be a casino, let the casino have all the appearance of a casino and let the casino have all the games guaranteed to create losers, to take candy from a baby, and in spite of all that make the 'sure thing' fail miserably. Let this failure be the mark of your success which you then sell as a brand which you paste on a building.

In some ways Trump is like an inverted Sisyphus. He stands at the top of the hill and when the boulder rolls up (in Trump's inverted world) he pushes it back down and declares victory. Crowds gather around to cheer him losing."

– Donal McGraith, Charivari Press blog post

37.

Somewhere in radio land some of the millions of people who believe a president who has told over 10,000 lies in office are listening. His latest effort being the big one, to destroy the United States.

Radio Voice Over

This is CUTS 105.5 FM.

Call-in Host

Don't be misled. Are the Iranians responsible for the Israeli self-defense attacks and Palestine occupation? Of course they are. It goes without saying.

Caller

You think they're behind this anti-Trump and commie propaganda getting pasted up all over town?

Call-in Host

Naw, I'm not saying that. More likely that's your typical angry Democrats. I'm just sayin' that there's a group of people with some big bucks behind all this garbage. Everything costs money.

Caller

A fake protest movement.

Call-in Host

Yeah, and one that appeals to socialists, angry women and Muslims advocating sharia law. Ya gotta be vigilant.

I wondered if "vigilant" was code for "vigilante". Sure enough, that night some white nationalist thought police adjuncts on patrol downtown grabbed a sixteen year old graffiti artist tagging a mailbox and beat the hell out of him. They left him laying, bleeding on the street, as "a lesson". As they curtailed his free speech, they yelled at him that they were defending America and the constitution.

The next morning was when Ted Fox began his series of cards – modeled on baseball cards – of the new breed of fascists, crypto-fascists, nationalists and reactionaries.

Of course Bolsonaro, Trump, Netanyahu, Le Pen, and Orbán got cards. Canadians Ford, Scheer and Kenney too. Britons Farage and Johnson headed a group from the UK dreaming of imperial glory. And America's most murderous psychopaths were there. Like Steven Miller (who likely thinks that turning Jews away to die in Nazi gas chambers was going too soft on them), Mike Pompeo and John Bolton, both busy at the time inventing pretexts to begin a war to slaughter Iranian children in the name of biblical prophecy and Saudi arms sales blessed by a god who is on their side.

Jair Bolsonaro
"the exterminator"

Annihilating the rainforest, democracy,
indigenous people, and all other humanity.

New Faces of Fascism Collector Cards
#7

"I cannot at present remember how it was that we struck upon this somewhat curious topic, as it was at that time, but I know we had a long discussion about Macpherson, Ireland, and Chatterton, and that with regard to the last I insisted that his so-called forgeries were merely the result of an artistic desire for perfect representation; that we had no right to quarrel with an artist for the conditions under which he chooses to present his work; and that all Art being to a certain degree a mode of acting, an attempt to realise one's own personality on some imaginative plane out of reach of the trammeling accidents and limitations of real life, to censure an artist for a forgery was to confuse an ethical with an aesthetical problem."
– Oscar Wilde, *The Portrait of Mr. W.H.*

38.

Since two weeks had now passed with no response from Davey, Keith approached Belle and she promised to do another poster and flyer using photos of the meth lab. This one would ratchet up the pressure on Davey.

The flyer took wing that night, distributed over the downtown core courtesy of a southwest wind, an intentionally unlocked door to an office building roof, and a graduate student living in a co-op high-rise.

Besides the photos, it advised that a video of the meth lab revealing its location was soon to be uploaded to You Tube if there was no response from the interested parties.

39.

The afternoon meeting was held at Tennessee Butler's ... let's just call it Animal Farm.

"The creatures outside looked from pig to man, and from man to pig, and from pig to man again; but already it was impossible to say which was which." (Orwell, Animal Farm)

No political figures nor James Ross III were present. It was only a partial get-together of the syndicate because it was precipitated by the posters showing the meth lab under Butler's barn.

Tennessee vigorously waved a trotter, pawing the air while snorting, "Could be Democrats behind it since they're going after you, Chief. Probably want some liberal bleeding heart police chief who's soft on crime. Have you asked the FBI for help?" Irony was not Tennessee's strong suit.

Chief of Police Bill (known as Stoner in his youth) Jackson shook his head with a twitch as if brushing away flies, and said, "Right now we're gonna deal with this locally. The last thing we want is the feds nosing around. We've got the word out and should get something soon on who has a grudge. I think you may be right. This could be political. There's a bunch of other shit going on and we don't know if it's connected. If it is, those responsible have access to some sophisticated printing equipment. That'll narrow it down.

"But what about you two? What the hell I want to know is how someone got a picture of what's under your barn? Don't you have CCTV? Anybody watch it?"

"We looked at the tapes," bleated four-legs-good Davey. "The intruder was there the same night the man called in to 9-1-1. It was pissing rain and all you can make out on it might as well have been a ghost. Just looked like a grey shadow so the guy watching the monitors missed it."

Stoner said. "Any chance this has something to do with your biker friends? It looks like whoever did this had some inside information."

"No, they're cool" squealed Butler in his best piggish bravado. "They don't rat each other out. We're like the Rosses and the police, a family. Loyalty above all. It's gotta be Davey's actor friend who's the rat."

"The posters are signed, 'The Irishman,' and that's his nickname," bleated two-legs-better Davey.

"So here's what we're gonna do," said the chief. "Take down the lab. Stash everything. Sanitize the place. Worst comes to worst and more stuff gets posted, or we get pressure, we can say the photograph was doctored and there's nothing in the barn. In the meantime," turning to Davey he said, "We assume this is your actor pal's doing. Give him a call, set up a meeting and we'll pick him up when he shows."

Davey called Zach immediately after the meeting. He agreed to Zach's demand to meet at Davey's place the next day. The meeting time was set for eleven a.m.

40.

Feeling caught in a maze with no means of escape, forever re-exploring the same pathways, Zach mentally prepared for what would happen once he turned himself in to the police. He had awful memories of juvenile detention. Still, he'd surrender himself, even if they were unsuccessful in substituting *The Japanese Fire Tree* for a forgery.

At 7:30 a.m. he and Keith left the latter's condo.

Zach had kept watch on Davey's apartment, peeking from behind Keith's curtains. Since Davey was still a no show it was deemed to be a safe assumption that he wouldn't be home until close to their scheduled meeting at eleven.

The visit was Keith's suggestion, made after a sudden inspiration. "Instead of watching for Davey and trying to go to his place as soon as he gets home, presumably without his biker friends, why don't we just put some of the photos of his dealing in smokes in a brown manila envelope and slide it under his door? And we can include a note telling him we aren't coming and to phone my number. When he does, we negotiate our silence for his help." It was a much safer option than waiting and hoping that Davey would be alone when he got home because it was just as likely that he'd show up for the meeting with some of his biker friends in tow.

The envelope was in Keith's backpack.

There was a cluster of three people near the building's street door, two elderly women were checking their mailboxes while, fortuitously, an old man stood frozen in the doorway, half in and half out, holding the door open, apparently on his way out when he decided to stop and talk.

Zach and Keith, dressed in ball caps, sunglasses, and sporting thin beards, slipped behind him through the open door without raising any questions or concern.

They took the elevator up to the third floor. At the door to Davey's unit, Keith set his backpack on the floor and squatted as he unzipped it.

Zach stepped forward and tried the door knob. It was locked but he removed a wire from his pocket and in perhaps twenty seconds the door swung open.

"What the fuck are you doing?" whispered Keith, standing.

"Just going to have a look around. Plus it'll make Davey more anxious if we leave the envelope on his kitchen table. He'll then know we can get to him any time we want."

Zach stepped through the door as Keith, shaking his head, stood and followed. After a momentary hesitation to allow the feelings of nausea to subside when hit with the aural wall of stale tobacco smoke and a soupçon of sweat, they did a brief recon. There was a cheap kitchen set in the dining room area, a sofa and TV stand with TV in the livingroom. The huge ashtray sitting on a coffee table was filled with butts and ashes that had spilled over its edges. There was a double mattress on the floor of the bedroom with some grubby looking sheets on it. Who knows what life-threatening adventures lay in store for our Lewis and Clark if they had reconnoitered into the bathroom? They took a pass.

Keith, his open backpack in hand, took out the envelope and laid it on the kitchen table. "Let's get out of here," he said. "This place is vile."

Zach either didn't hear or care, still absorbed in his examination of the disarranged premises. He made a quick trip to the front window and pulled the curtains back just enough to glance outside. As he turned around a sheet of paper laying on the coffee table caught his eye. He walked over to take a closer look. "Whoa! Have a look at this?"

Keith rolled his eyes and sighed with frustration but obeyed. On it was written, "James back door Kaden." That was followed by a series of numbers and symbols. Below that was written, "Security 3-6-5-5"

Keith glanced quizzically at Zach who said, "There's Kaden locks on the doors of James Ross's house. It's why I had to smash my way in. They're supposed to be impregnable because of some unique system they use. This looks to be the pass code to unlock the back door. The other number's the security code to deactivate the alarm once you're inside."

"Jesus. So with this we could just walk into Ross's house?"

"Looks like. Just walk in."

"Why would Davey have it?"

"He's a gopher. A flunkie and errand runner. He probably does stuff for James Ross besides kissing his ass."

"So what do you think? Should we still leave the photos?"

"No way. And tell him we were here? Grab the envelope. We can get to the painting without his help and after the switch we can post the photographs." He added with swelled chest, frontier justice fighter, "We're going to use the pics to expose all those fuckers."

GRADE 3 REPORT CARD

Child's Name ________________________________

Day's Absent 200+ (playing golf instead of working)

Subject	Grade	Comments
Geography	F	Nambia (with or without an "increasingly self-sufficient" health system) is not a country. Nor is "Whales" (with or without a prince).
History	F	Review material on (the late!) Frederick Douglass. Still waiting on your map of the airports taken over by the Continental Army.
Science	F	The moon is not part of Mars. That it is cold in winter does not disprove global warming. (Storms are indeed "very wet" though.)
Health	F	Windmills do not cause cancer. Lying about your height does not make you less obese. Cheeseburgers are not a health food.
Physical Education	F	We are not born with a finite amount of energy that makes all exercise misguided (except for golf). Stop driving your golf cart on greens!
Mathematics	F	Two trillion dollar budget mistakes are unacceptable. Mexico is not paying for your wall through the USMCA or by any other means.

Comments

Donald is far less mature than other Grade 3 students.

Demonstrates the following unacceptable behaviors for a big boy.

- Constant name calling.

- Needing pictures in his reading / short attention span.

- Bullying.

- Bragging about non-existent achievements. Know-it-all attitude.

- Incessant TV watching.

- Daily consumption of fast food.

- Needing to be the center of attention at all times.

- Temper tantrums about the most minor of things.

- Non-stop lying. Inventing boogeymen to frighten gullible children.

- Inability to handle criticism.

- Inappropriate touching of females.

- Outsized sense of entitlement.

- Cannot distinguish between himself and the world.

- Lack of empathy and inability to abide by basic moral precepts.

- Excessive laziness.

- Trying to con the other children out of their money.

- Writing his surname in very large letters on everything.

- Obsession with money and shiny objects. Showing off baubles.

- Inability to recognize that he is wrong about many things.

Parent's Signature: _______________________________________

41.

"They're packing up," said Zach from atop his stool – an old tree trunk in the bush behind the James Ross mansion.

The three people behind him said nothing. Like Zach, they wore hoodies and masks. Keith's car was hidden in the bush.

"Okay, they've driven off," Zach said eventually, turning to address his guerrillas. "Remember. The place has motion detectors around it. Davey told me, when I went in the front, that I had ten minutes from the time I tripped one until the cops arrived. So, we've got to stay together and move fast."

He said, "1-2-3 Go!" and they raced across the yard as a group.

Zach, using the security codes they'd found that morning, went to work on the Kaden lock and the alarm. He had the group inside the house within thirty seconds.

Zach, since he knew the layout, went to the front window to keep watch while Keith remained at the back door doing the same. Belle and Donal went to the study. They removed *The Japanese Fire Tree* from the wall, lay it on the floor, and Belle immediately went to work snapping photographs, measuring, taking notes and video taping. After, three to four minutes, she scraped off some minute samples of paint and scanned the painting with a portable ultra-violet lamp because Donal had urged her to do some rudimentary tests to determine the age of the painting.

Meanwhile, Donal walked through the house. He did a quick tour of the "art gallery" in the main rooms. Returning to the study he spent some time examining a painting of flowers hanging on another wall of the study. And just before they left he had a look at the blueprints on James III's desk.

"I'm done!" Belle called out for everyone's edification and they assembled at the back door.

Belle, Donal, and Keith ran for the bush while Zach rearmed the alarm and the door. As he reached the bush he heard the police sirens in the distance.

A few minutes later they were wheeling their way back to town. The whole thing had gone off perfectly.

"Can I ask what those papers were on the desk?" Belle said, turning her head to take in Donal in the back seat.

"They were blueprints for something called The Teresa Ross Memorial Art Gallery."

"A new gallery?"

"Not only that, but apparently a private gallery to be built in the lot adjacent to his house. That's why the surveyors."

"A private gallery," said Belle, her words then slowed as she worked out her thoughts, "but that could mean that the gallery he's going to donate the painting to will be his own."

"Right," said Donal. "He can get a tax break in the millions for donating to himself and then use the gallery as if it's part of his home to entertain his wealthy guests."

"Nice trick," said Zach.

"And it's not just that," Donal continued. "That painting I was looking at in the study is also by Schiele. And there are two smaller Schieles in the livingroom. Ross has been buying Schiele landscapes and it wouldn't surprise me if this whole thing is a scam to jack up the prices of all of them."

"There's something else," said Belle. "There was blue fluorescence visible when I used the ultra-violet light."

There was a pause, as if waiting to deliver a punchline.

"And?" said Keith.

"It means that the painting is a forgery since it was painted with an oil paint that wasn't invented until thirty years after it was supposed to have been painted."

"I.R.S. rules allow plenty of leeway. Private operating foundations, tax experts note, can qualify for a tax exemption even without letting in a single visitor. Tax-exempt organizations can also fulfill their mission by lending out works, giving grants or making the collection available to researchers ...

Once a nonprofit foundation is set up, it can write off the cost of conserving, caring for and insuring the art, as well as designing and building exhibition and storage facilities."
– Patricia Cohen, 'Writing Off The Warhol Next Door'

42.

*She arose in the dark on the day of the dawn execution —
as if the timing of a state killing was some honored tradition
that must be followed — and she made the hundred mile
journey to the penitentiary.*

*There is no time so lonesome as the middle of the night
when, alone, you come face to face with your own mortality
and fears.*

*Blanche drove past the last house of the prison town when,
on impulse, about three hundred yards before the
penitentiary gates, she veered her car off the highway and on*

to a dirt spur. She stopped the car but remained inside while it idled.

The spur was once the start of a road, going somewhere, to a clearing where firewood for the prison would be delivered and stored, but the road was now just two overgrown ruts going nowhere, except to a teen make out spot known locally as, "the road to ruin".

She wanted to be a singer and actress, like the women she watched on TV who went south and became big stars. Everyone recognized them. She'd moved here to make that happen. Unfortunately her singing voice was too weak and thin, but she continued to practice four hours a day. She began to fret about missing practice time but didn't consider leaving having long ago decided that she must attend the execution out of respect for the victim's children.

I'll look away at the crucial moment, she told herself.

Her knees bounced violently.

Six years earlier she'd witnessed a murder after one of her gigs, as she was leaving a particularly seedy roadhouse. She saw a woman named Ellen Hart shoot a resisting robbery target who also happened to be an off duty cop. During her interrogation Hart said how she owed the guy one, so it was deemed to be first degree murder.

Blanche was compelled to testify and to her horror, as an opponent of the death penalty, her testimony led to Hart's sentence of execution.

Blanche had thought this day would never happen but Ellen Hart, refusing a prolonged life of depression and isolation while waiting to die, declined to appeal the decision and asked for a speedy execution.

"In due time," the state said, beginning Hart's six year

torture of solitary confinement while there was an official determination of whether the prisoner was of sound enough mind to opt for death and a release from pain. As if a sane person would deny the inevitable.

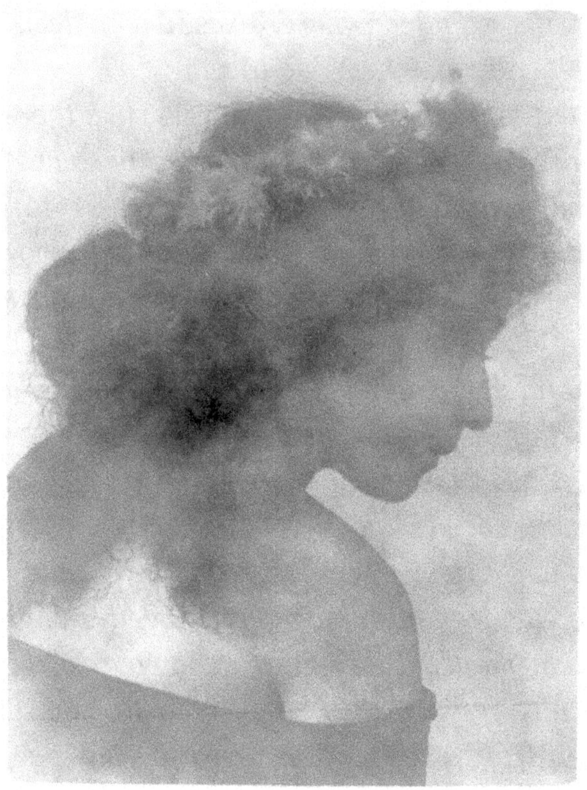

The state's real rationale for the delay, according to writer Jean-Guy Talbot and some other critics, was so that Hart couldn't deprive decent, god fearing people of the right to kill her at a time of their own choosing.

Blanche had come to deeply regret having testified, even though, over the years, the local paper had featured story after story about the murdered policeman, painting him as a saint, with photos of his grieving wife and children.

Law and order editorials accompanied each story.

In the past year, a news web site had finally decided to look further into what Hart had meant when she said of the police officer that she "owed" him; an implied allegation dismissed as baseless during the trial and ignored in the mainstream media. But new witnesses had come forward and a case was being built on Hart's behalf. It was only then that the state decided the time was right to execute her.

The courts, the police, the prison system with its unspeakable horrors, all became sources of dread in Blanche's mind. A mindless and moral-free steamroller once set in motion.

On the front seat of Blanche's car was an old felt pennant with the name of a mid-western town on it and a graphic of a field of corn. She'd bought it at a flea market the day before. It was the sort that, years before, a boy or girl would have tacked to their bedroom wall to show that they were a world traveler, although all their pennants were from towns within a hundred mile radius. Fellow dreamers.

The moisture from Blanche's hands had freed the felt's green dye. Looking down, seeing that it had stained her skirt, she violently threw the pennant to the floor of the car.

She looked up to see a sheriff's van drive past, going in the direction of the prison. Blanche couldn't see inside the van but was certain that it carried Ellen Hart who was housed at the women's prison.

What must she be thinking?

Blanche opened the car window and could hear faint yelling from a group of protesters at the prison gates.

"We are now in modern times," Blanche said aloud, to no one and for who knows what reason.

Did I say that or did I hear it? She began to weep.

She turned on the radio, rotated the dial until she reached a college station, and the sound of Iris Dement singing 'Wasteland of the Free' filled the car.

While we sit gloating in our greatness
justice is sinking to the bottom of the sea
Living in the wasteland of the free.

Blanche gazed skyward and then floated up, right up out of the car and over the prison gates. She looked down at the building roofs.

When she got home that evening Blanche immediately began to pack to return home to the north.

A week after that she was in the psychiatric ward where she met Zach, and in a PTSD group where she made the acquaintance of Keith.

Blanche's bond had been set at six figures which was beyond everyone's financial means, including that of her parents. So Blanche remained at the city jail while awaiting trial. The police had been stymied by her refusal to talk about who was behind the political vandalism occurring around the downtown area.

Blanche had had regular visits from Keith, Stella, and Billie, her friend from work.

She'd never bought into the cant about wage labor being ennobling and fulfilling. She preferred her freedom. For brief moments she could become engrossed in something at work and pleased with whatever results she accomplished, but it didn't take away from the fact that she only worked for others in order to survive and from a lack of other options. It was penal servitude. Wage slavery. FREEDOM IS SLAVERY. Answerable to bosses whose only skill lay in convincing their bosses that they had pulled off significant improvements (but whose projects were flops). It was – like Donald Trump slashing environmental protections and then claiming to be the savior of the environment – palpable nonsense yet believed by those too ignorant to know the difference. Being a charlatan and a liar was obviously the road to success.

Her one compensation at work was Billie, who was a wonderful writer and musician. When Billie visited Blanche in jail they spent time living their fantasy vacation to somewhere warm. It wasn't about consumption and leisure anymore, nor to have sexual adventures with strangers away from the judgmental eyes of family with their expectations of good girl behaviour. It was an expression of a loving and close friendship that had developed between the two of them in a poorly paid job where there was solidarity; the only decent thing about menial labor. The beach and the south were about warmth, and sun, and ease, and companionship.

"You look like you got some sleep at last," said Stella, during her final visit.

"Sometimes exhaustion takes over," said Blanche. "It's a relief because the middle of the night is the worst time, almost unbearable. There are women yelling, crying, and banging on things. The guards can be quite insensitive."

Both women glanced over at the sallow face of a watching guard. There was always someone watching.

"Something is going to happen soon," said Stella. "Please don't get too down. The 'thing' I've mentioned could be a day or two away and then Zach will give himself up. I think everything will change then."

Blanche said, "I hope so." She'd moved to a mental rapprochement with Zach and chosen not to continue to be angry with him, or doubt him. They were in this together.

"Oh, he again told me to tell you he's sorry. This trouble is all his fault and he's going to get you out of it."

Stella wished that she could change places with Blanche but declined to say so lest it sound hollow, something easily said that did nothing except to boost one's heroic illusions. Instead, she changed the subject and told Blanche about the new plans for her bakery.

"Kalie's involved. There's a year left on the lease and she's going to keep up with the rent payments so we can re-open. It won't be selling baking anymore though. I hope our recent activism gets some people thinking and helps to facilitate a wide movement, but every initiative also counts and contributes to change."

"What are you going to sell? Stuff gothic and macabre?" She smiled.

"No. Nothing. Everything will be free but I'll take donations. I plan to invite people to bring in their baking so it can be given away. We're going to do information sheets on consuming less, growing your own food, running a business to benefit people rather than to make money. And I'll start a gift list. If someone needs a toaster, for instance, we can put it up on a bulletin board list, but not give out the person's name. If anyone has a toaster they can give away, or is willing to barter, they can respond or bring one in. The possibilities are endless."

43.

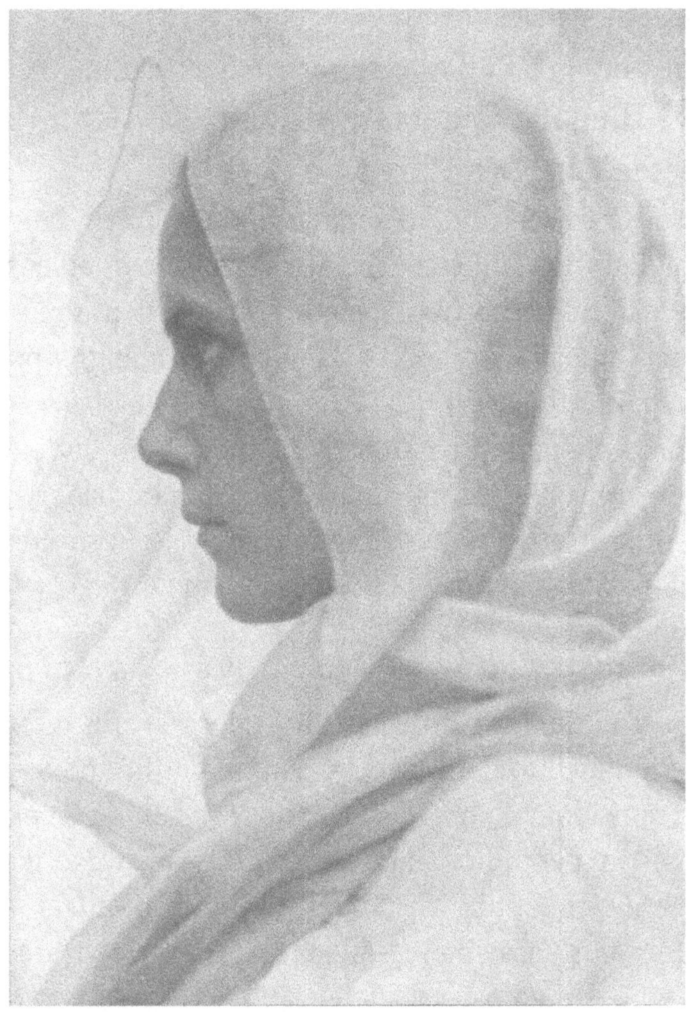

The posters done by Belle were small: 8.5"x14"
The top half of the poster featured the headline:

Tennessee Butler's Meth Lab

Two photographs followed: one of the lab at Butler's and
the other of his barn. A paragraph of text provided links to a
blog and a YouTube video promising a video that would

demonstrate, conclusively, the location of the lab as well as the involvement of the police and Chief Jackson in the operation.

On the bottom half of the poster ran the headline:

The Illegal Cigarette Business Run From Tennessee Butler's Farm

It also followed the mixed media approach combining photographs with links to social media and media sharing postings. (It had been anticipated correctly that some of the social media postings would be pulled down as the powerful wielded their influence.)

The only photo and bit of video exposing an outlet selling illegal cigarettes was the shop near Stella's bakery where Zach had been given a hard time. There had been no will to out small shop owners but Zach had insisted on this exception.

Getting the posters up had been a well-organized effort to set off alarms and create other diversions while the posters were being glued to mail, newspaper, and utility boxes. It had required considerable bravery. But not everything went well.

One of the people posting, Janet McLean, was taken into custody. She was known to police as a political activist although in this case she was actually just a friend of a friend helping with some posters.

I'd have thought that she might be given a ticket or a slap on the wrist but for political prisoners of any severity, in the city of the Ross family, Room 101 was waiting.

Janet was brow beaten for information about who was engaging in the latest activism. Threatening to go after one's family to get compliance was, of course, a utilized tactic in the time honored American tradition. Love for anyone other than Big Brother was your undoing.

Janet was creatively charged not only with minor offenses, like defacing public property, but with resisting arrest and assaulting a police officer. In total, she was facing up to twenty years in a maximum security prison if found guilty on all counts. This is a form of torture.

A video tape of the arrest showed conclusively that Janet was the one who'd been assaulted despite the absence of any resistance on her part. Still, if the thing went to a jury of indoctrinated sheep who relied on authority to lay out reality for them, one could expect that the police version of events would be believed in spite of the fact that her only crime was to dissent.

We hoped that the charges were merely a ploy to try and leverage names and information from Janet.

44.

The real blockbuster poster and media effort came the following day. It was explosive because it accused a pillar of the community of criminal acts.

The headline read:

How To Forge An Egon Schiele Painting In The Post-Truth Age

This time, the posters were huge: 3'x5' The same size as the family images of past residents, posted earlier. The poster itself was broken up into six blocks. Each was numbered and the first five contained one segment of a pictorial essay. The last block listed URLs.

Only fifteen installations were put up and all were over bus shelter ads. Amazingly no one was caught. Until now, these billboards had mostly been used by street artists détourning them for political satire, defacing a luxury car ad with graffiti reading "hope is the leash of submission" for example.

The poster made some surmises with respect to the actions of James Ross III (now widely accepted as being correct). Together its five blocks laid out the steps needed to forge a Schiele painting, and included a photograph.

The sectional texts read:

1. Be James Ross III. Obtain a forged Egon Schiele painting entitled *The Japanese Fire Tree*.
2. Pay a noted "art expert" a whack of under the table money to validate it as authentic. Have it appraised at a ludicrous amount for more under the table money.
3. Pay someone desperate for money to stage a mock robbery of your house. (Do this through the help of your friend Tennessee Butler.) Retrieve the painting

from the "robber" and approach the insurance company posing as the thief. When they "buy" the painting back from you for millions – a fraction of the appraised value – give your cronies a cut.

4. Claim you knew nothing about it when the robber, through a fluke, gets caught. Let them spend their life in prison although they were told they were retrieving a valueless painting in a domestic dispute. Announce that you are donating the work to a gallery to keep it safe (and enjoy being feted as a saint).

5. Neglect to mention that the gallery is a private gallery being built adjacent to your house. In this way no one will ever look too closely at the painting, and you can get huge tax rebates for the donation while keeping the painting in what amounts to a personal party room. Get further tax breaks to cover the insurance, maintenance, and construction of your private gallery.

Photographs of the blueprint for the new gallery were posted online.

A video of ultraviolet light being shone on the painting was uploaded along with an explanation of what the visible blue fluorescence proved.

There was no attempt to disguise the fact that a group of masked intruders had been in the James Ross mansion illegally. In fact, this proved that the painting in the videos was *The Japanese Fire Tree*.

In another video, Zach, utilizing his celebrity, narrated his personal story of *The Japanese Fire Tree* theft. He was a star again. It was video taped, posted online, and copied onto DVDs which were mailed to a number of news and scandal organizations around the country.

Fox News, of course, featured that "explosive" (Dink Links, The Tribune) news story of how James Ross had been the victim of a liberal conspiracy.

45.

This episode in Keith's life (it was a year before the theft of *The Japanese Fire Tree*) is one for another day but it needs mentioning here because it impacted later events.

Keith, for the fourth time that month, had been hiding in the woods near the nursing home owned by Douglas Ross. It was one of Keith's first attempts to shadow the wealthy and spy on them. It was a project to take photographs of the powerful doing disgusting things, (he would soon after put the project on the back burner until he had enough photographs to do a major article).

Douglas was the younger brother of James Ross III. He'd been an exile from the family for a number of years while he was in and out of psychiatric care suffering from depression,

alcoholism, drug addiction, impulse control problems, mental instability and borderline personality disorder.

Douglas, it was whispered by people who knew the family, was most likely an outcome of too much inbreeding among the British aristocracy. Eventually, heavily medicated and back in the Ross fold, his father gave Douglas the funds to purchase the nursing home.

He now seemed to be doing well. He was in a serious relationship with one of the nurses and – so they said – headed for the altar.

Keith had met Douglas during his stay in the psychiatric unit and the pair had conversed. Douglas was deeply resentful about what he deemed to be a lack of family support, and even more than that, of the success of his brother James. Douglas seemed to crave attention.

He told Keith that when he and James were young, growing up on his father's estate, that he (Douglas) used to poison the frogs in the local pond after he would catch them. He thought it was funny. It was power over life and death that thrilled him, he said.

Keith speculated that this was why Douglas decided to study nursing.

Douglas though, considered himself to be a fundamentalist Christian so found rationalizations for killing: robbers, criminals, "threats" to Israel, and so on. A deep streak of self-righteous intolerance was always on display.

Keith obviously didn't know what to expect when he began to stake out the nursing home in the evenings. He suspected that he might catch Douglas acting true to form in some way, contradicting his public persona.

Keith camped out behind the nursing home near an area

where people smoked. He'd seen some nurses having a quick snog on more than one occasion.

The high frequency of corpses being removed from the facility in the night gradually seeped into Keith's consciousness. It seemed to be an inordinate amount, even for a nursing home filled with the elderly.

On one occasion, the chief of police was filmed having a smoke with Douglas beside the back door of the nursing home in the middle of the night while a corpse on a gurney was being carted away behind them.

They were smiling and talking. It struck Keith as odd behaviour for a cop given that he was apparently at the home because of an unexplained death. But, at the time, Keith wasn't someone to suspect the police of wrong doing.

Keith began to film the pair and, at one point, inadvertently coughed. Douglas and Stoner Jackson both spun in his direction, alarmed apparently at being observed.

The chief strode towards the woods in Keith's direction but the latter high-tailed it and managed to evade Stoner.

Keith left off his visits to the nursing home after that but now, one year later, the place again began to occupy his thoughts.

46.

James Ross stood in front of Tennessee Butler and Stoner Jackson. They were in III's kitchen, but anywhere this group met had the moral stench of a barnyard slaughterhouse.

"How did these people, these lowlife break and enter specialists, know the codes to get into my house?" James said. He paused and looked away, the sound of his deep voice was still reverberating in his skull cavity, so he had to bask in its perfection. He went on, "The information had to come from Davey because he was the only person besides me who knows those codes."

"But why would he tip them off?" said Butler.

"My guess would be that the thieves threatened to expose his cigarette racket if he didn't help them get that woman out of jail."

"But they ratted out Davey's business with their posters."

"Yeah. Davey's a traitor and stupid to boot. He'd never ask himself why the actor and his friends would honor their word about keeping silent once they got what they wanted?"

"No honor among thieves," intoned the noted ironist Tennessee Butler while sadly shaking his head at the treachery of mankind.

"And the group knew to bring an ultraviolet light. You have to remember too that there were only three people who knew the painting was a forgery, and about the paint. You Tennessee, myself and Davey. Now I give you a pass so they had to have gotten the information from Davey."

Turning to Stoner Jackson, who'd been sitting quietly throughout the meeting, his tough sheriff's pose locked in, James said off-handedly, "And what about the woman you have in custody? You can't really hold her now."

Jackson looked at him severely. "You want to admit the painting is a forgery and let her go? That'll make you look like a crook!"

"I don't want this coming out in court. As far as we're concerned, if the painting is a forgery then we knew nothing about it and the idea that we were conducting a scam is nonsense."

"But you want me to let that liberal lowlife out of jail?"

"Yeah. Say it's because you confirmed the painting was a

forgery. When she's out, take care of her. Take care of Davey too. And for god's sake deal with Zach Lennox so he stops running his mouth off. None of them can talk to the FBI. Maybe we can fake a story that the couple fucked off together with the real painting. Maybe make them suspects in whatever happens to Davey. Get creative. They were a gang perhaps. Make sure people know about Davey's lengthy criminal record.

"Oh, and take the FBI, if they investigate, on a tour of the basement of the barn after you've made sure the place is scoured clean." After a pause, he stared off into the distance once again to show off his magnificent profile and have it admired, adding, "I'll do a ton of media containment and PR."

"Um. There's more to this," the chief said, looking at III. Someone, somehow got on to what's been going on with Douglas. Maybe they're just shooting in the dark, but the head nurse at the home had a call asking for information on the rate of deaths of people in their care. This could get real ugly. Last year someone was spying on Douglas and me outside the home after one of the deaths. They even took a picture of us together."

"That's not my problem," said James. "I told you not to help him cover anything up. I'm sure you'll find a way to deal with things. You always do."

"And if not, I sure as hell do," Tennessee Butler oinked.

James, still looking at Stoner, said, "Maybe you could leak some names to the freedom fighters; the names of your suspects behind all the disgraceful propaganda being pasted up around town and let them do some housecleaning."

"Way ahead of you" grunted Stoner, with a smirk.

47.

The farce of examining *The Japanese Fire Tree* and declaring it to be a forgery played out over the next few days.

While that was happening there were over a dozen instances of violence against people suspected by the police of having taken part in the "anti-social activities" (Dink Winks, The Tribune) of the previous few weeks. None of the attacks against suspected activists seemed to have been committed by the police themselves so were obviously the result of intelligence being passed on to the alt-right gangs.

As activists were attacked or intimidated, they fled the city. And who could blame them? It was a question of life and death.

I, for one, would never have envisioned the retaliatory violence that happened – but perhaps I never imagined how much of a threat that we would become (although people with no scruples, when backed into a corner, behave as expected). Perhaps my surprise is a reflection of naivety.

Stella's bakery and the print shop

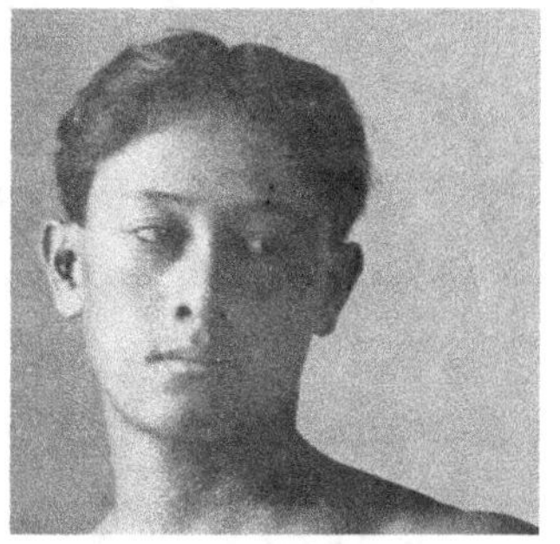

next door were burned to the ground one night when, fortunately, the pair were away visiting Stella's family.

The names, addresses, and phone numbers of all suspected activists had been posted online so even though Stella and Kalie were out of town they were still subject to the anonymous phone calls, homophobic rants, threats, and racism from "the city's finest examples of American manhood out protecting freedom" (warning poster with 30's fascist art being posted by the alt-right gangs).

The day after the fire, Kalie and Stella left for the farm of some friends of the former. They were welcome to stay there as long as they pulled their weight.

Belle did a huge water paint mural on the wall of her factory squat. The painting replicated *The Japanese Fire Tree*. She got word out that her squat would be the location of a huge party to celebrate. It was promoted with the catchy slogan: "Dance to the end of reality".

Over seven hundred people showed up but it wasn't until after 2:00 a.m. that the militias and police figured out what was happening.

The squat was swarmed by the alt-right gangs and then by the police to "restore order". The combined attack became known as "The End of the World Riot" (Blinky Bink, The Tribune) as those attacked were directly blamed for their own head bashings and branded as criminals. Forty-two people were arrested and twenty-six of the partiers were injured. Nineteen militia and three police were as well.

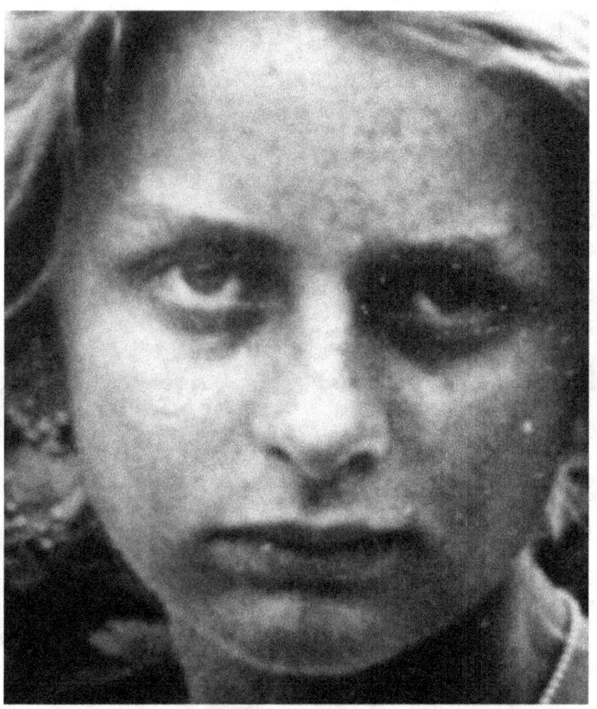

Blanche was released from jail and within three hours was on a plane with Billie to a beach somewhere. She didn't even go home, certain by now that her condo would be watched.

She'd arranged a loan from her parents to be paid off after she sold her condo. She did manage a phone call to Zach however, to explain her plan. They agreed to meet in another city in two weeks time.

Throughout the purge Zach had remained hidden at Keith's. He'd somehow escaped detection by the police, likely because Keith wasn't a known liberal.

Keith had repeatedly criticized Zach for not going to visit Blanche after it had been publicly revealed that *The Japanese Fire Tree* was a forgery – even telling him that he should be out shopping at a sports store for "a bigger set of balls" – but Zach was a survivor. He left town the day after Blanche, wearing a disguise and acting up a storm. He picked up his car near Billie's where Blanche had left it earlier.

Keith remained in the city determined to investigate Douglas Ross's nursing home. Maybe, he fantasized, he'd find a beautiful nurse there who'd help him.

48.

Lemony rapped softly on the door of Davey's apartment. Lemony was civilized after all, a man of culture, plus there was no need to alert the neighbors to his presence.

Kenny looked at Lemony with more than his usual lack of comprehension, mystified by the soft knock. Kenny may have put it down to weakness or timidity because he raised his hand and delivered three resounding raps that could have raised the dead.

"Jesus," said Lemony under his breath, with resignation.

"What is it?" said a gruff voice from within the apartment, muted by the sound of the door.

In his usual speaking voice, in spite of the fact that the pleased with himself looking Kenny, beside him, had already announced their presence to half the building, Lemony said, "It's me Lemony, Davey. We need to talk."

"Fuck," said Davey to himself, but audible in the hallway as he opened the door. Maybe he could talk himself out of a beating. He opened the door a crack and peeked at Lemony.

"We need to talk," said Lemony.

Do people know they're going to die on the day they do?

I would suppose they don't if it's unexpected, otherwise they'd resist. When I hear about an unexpected death I sometimes picture the person getting up that morning, having a shower, getting dressed, and proceeding unawares to their death as if it was just another day.

Photos taken in the thirties, of smiling Europeans, have a haunted feel.

"Today is a good day to die." That phrase was made

famous by Black Elk but it was originally uttered by Low Dog apparently. Such acceptance for the naturalness of death.

I don't feel any anxiety about my impending demise. It's nature's way. Nature needs to change and adapt. We can't accumulate. We're all mistakes, prototypes in development. Forever. To linger on is against the way of the world.

In any case, this was the gist of my thoughts that day after hearing that Davey had been murdered.

It happened in the late evening.

People,
a fallen people,
dead-of-heart, dazed and lonely,
beneath the sinister burden of their own corpses,
wandered from exile to exile,
the aching lust for crime sweltering in their hands.
– Farugh Farrokhzad, *Earthly Verses*

Keith, as he did on most nights, stood at his third floor condo window with his right hand resting on the waist high cross-frame while staring out through the darkness. He was watching a woman in the apartment building directly across the road. She was reading. He would often watch her while she read.

He abruptly jumped back when some indefinable dark matter plummeted past the woman's window. Stumbling backwards against a chair, Keith gripped its back for support. The projectile outside was indiscernible as anything but a blurry mass, yet human nature had recognized impending death and instinctively recoiled.

Keith did not approach the window and look down.

Instead, he turned his face towards a nearby bookshelf crammed full of books about photography.

There was no audible sound on the third floor when the lump struck the pavement below but a scream soon confirmed it was a body. This was followed by yelling, muffled, and barely audible to Keith.

He turned his face back toward the window. His expression was now serene, as if bodies falling from the heavens required no more empathy than what was expended on heavy rain or some other fact of nature.

By morning the media would be broadcasting the names and images of Blanche and Zach, "persons of interest" in the city's latest murder. Everyone knew what that meant.

49.

At the White House, Ivanka is asking "Daddy" to take her along on a meeting. The photos from it will be helpful in her 2024 presidential bid, she says.

Daddy has to remind her, "Baby, the people are going to come together and demand that I serve a third term because I'm doing so well."

"That would be wonderful," she replies, "2028 then."

In the state senate there are cheers to celebrate the unanimous passage of another bill to stop environmental activism by calling it "violence against critical infrastructure".

At The Tribune office a local reporter is typing out his story about the "crazed radicals" who invaded the downtown. Of course he is speaking about liberals. The previous evening 150 white supremacists had marched downtown with banners that read, "taking back the streets." (I expect that at any moment the President will tweet about what fine people they are.) They paraded with their ugly chants, solemnity, self-importance, and tiki torches. But they were not alone. Not conceding the streets, over 800 people staged a rapidly organized counter march. Had the police not surrounded the white supremacists, things may have become violent.

There is much to be said for the street art, posters, and exposés set off by the plan to fake *The Japanese Fire Tree*. Questioning official truth must occur to stir people to action.

I, meanwhile, am looking into Stella and Kalie's idea to open a store that helps people to consume less and to share what they have with others. "The possibilities are endless," said Stella about local efforts to expand autonomy and community. I hope so. Every endeavor makes a difference.

"The cant of our political theater, the ridiculous obsessions over vice presidential picks or celebrity gossip that dominate the news industry, effectively masks the march toward corporate totalitarianism. The corporate state has convinced the masses, in essence, to clamor for their own enslavement.,..

The charade of junk politics is there not to offer a choice but to divert the crowd while our corporate masters move relentlessly forward, unimpeded by either party, to turn all dissent into a crime."

– Chris Hedges, 'Criminalizing Dissent'

50.

After *The Japanese Fire Tree* was determined absolutely to be a forgery, James Ross's insurance company insisted on obtaining confirmation of the authenticity of *Wildflowers*. They engaged two "art experts" for this task and they both decided that it too was a forgery. And who could doubt the word of an art expert? Or two? There was no gallery stamp on the back of the painting, nor was there any documentation of the sales history and there was no customs documentation.

While the paint used was not in question there were just too many other problems, like "stylistic inconsistency". James Ross the Second had no memory of the painting's acquisition so as far as anyone knew the work was likely acquired from the same individual who'd sold his grandfather *The Japanese Fire Tree*. At the heart of things was the fact that the experts didn't want to appear to be in the pocket of James Ross by validating a painting with zero provenance even though the painting was one of the rare specimens that appeared to be legitimate after scientific testing.[2]

James Ross the Third stood looking out the window of his study at the construction of the Teresa Ross Memorial Art Gallery going on nearby. If authentic, *Wildflowers* would have been worth tens of millions of dollars – a real blow – but James still had plenty of other artwork to make the gallery worth his while.

The cleaning lady, Roberta, was just finishing up her dusting. Turning to leave she said, "Excuse me Mr. Ross. I noticed the two paintings that you took down." The paintings were leaning against a wall. "Is there somewhere you'd like

____

2 According to Switzerland's Fine Arts Expert Institute chief Yann Walther, "approximately 70–90 percent of artworks that his organization examines on behalf of collectors and dealers end up not being by the artist claimed" – artnet News, October 13, 2014

me to put them?"

James half turned his head, sure that his profile against the backdrop of the sky outside was quite impressive, and said, "I suppose you can put them somewhere in the basement Roberta. The one is a worthless forgery and the other seems to be as well. And if it isn't it may as well be since I can't insure it, sell it, or put it in the new gallery."

"Such a shame, especially the one of the wildflowers. So beautiful. It reminds me of the fields surrounding the house where I grew up. It was in the country near here. My sister and I would chase down butterflies there." What Roberta didn't mention was that the house was now gone except for traces of the stone foundation that had been built by her great-grandfather. An enormous lilac bush provided a ghostly reminder that a house had once stood on the spot. The forest that surrounded the house was now barren terrain having been clear cut by Ross Lumber. The small animal population, like the raccoons, had migrated into the city.

James watched the woman for a brief moment. Since he had never been known for his largess or empathy, what came next was entirely unexpected. "Why don't you take the thing then," he said impulsively. "It has no value to me. Since it has some sentimental value to you, you may as well have it. It's a little amateurish anyway." This was an opinion of recent vintage.

"Oh, Mr Ross, seriously?"

"Yes."

"That would be wonderful. Thank you. I'll put it in my livingroom (James Ross flinched at the thought that something of his would be hung in a plebeian house) and I'll put the other painting in your basement."

51.

April, 1912

On a day shortly before Egon's arrest, Wally looked around the studio in Neulengbach, at the several works of teenage girls in various stages of undress. The girls seemed to float on the page, unattached to furnishings or any other distracting indication of location. The entire focus was on the sensual subject.

"Egon," she said finally, "what happened to the beautiful painting of the wildflowers?"

"I sold it this morning."

"Didn't you plan to offer it to Osthaus? I gathered from what you said…"

"That was my intention but I hadn't yet written to him about it. And then a man came here this morning. An exporter he said he was. He'd seen me in the fields the other day, and asked to see the painting. He insisted that I sell it to him on the spot because he was on his way to America to live and wanted the painting because it reminded him of the countryside around here. This is where he grew up. He said that he was shipping his household furnishings tomorrow and the easiest thing for him would be to send the painting along with them."

"How lovely that the painting will be on the wall of someone who loves it rather than a collector or art market speculator."

"Yes, I thought so too."

Author's Note

The characters in this book are not modeled on specific individuals. They are compendiums of traits associated with various types. Egon and Wally are, of course, a bit of historical fiction.

Obviously, producing this book, this commodity, is a hypocritical action considering the views expressed within. It does, however, recycle the work of many people in new ways. One such case is the novel by Craig Grimes entitled, *The Aching Lust for Crime*.

I hope that anything needing to be cited has been. I make no claim to originality regarding many of the ideas expressed by characters or the narrator. I haven't cited sources for ideas that I've seen expressed by multiple people in the alternative press, or arrived at on my own and then seen stated by others. The principal sources that I read were: The Guardian, Truthout, Truthdig, The Decarie Report, Democracy Now, Al Jazeera English, Donal McGraith, Robert Reich, and Noam Chomsky.

In no cases (except for Egon Schiele and Wally Neuzil) are photographs meant to serve as illustrations of the characters. I apologize if there are any unsavory biographical details about individual photographers or subjects that I didn't know about (unless the unsavory characteristic of the subject was the reason for including the photograph).

Photo Credits

Unless otherwise noted, the graphics used came from two public domain sources. 1. The Silver Sheet (**SS**) 2. Ladies Home Journal Wyeth, N. C. (Newell Convers), 1882-1945 (**LHJ**)
Here are the license links for Creative Commons photos. They are published here under the same licenses:
CC0 1.0 – https://creativecommons.org/publicdomain/zero/1.0/ deed.en
CC BY-SA 2.0 – https://creativecommons.org/licenses/by-sa/2.0/deed.en
CC By 2.0 – https://creativecommons.org/licenses/by/2.0/
CC By 3.0 – https://creativecommons.org/licenses/by/ 3.0/deed.en
CC BY-SA 3.0 DE – https://creativecommons.org/licenses/by-sa/3.0/de/ deed.en

Cover: Public Domain. Thomas Eakins. https://tinyurl.com/y5p2vtsy
Frontispiece: Public Domain. Egon Schiele. Self-Portrait with Physalis. https://tinyurl.com/y5cl2nl5
Cast List: Public Domain. SS. https://tinyurl.com/y3t633dw
Part 1: Public Domain. Egon Schiele. Self-portrait. https://tinyurl.com/y3mkxsfy
Page 1: CC By 2.0 (license link above). Dustin Gaffke. https://tinyurl.com/y4bdn2bp
Page 3: Public Domain. Angrylambie. https://tinyurl.com/yyvepn4n
Page 4: Public Domain. Edward Burne-Jones. King Cophetua and the Beggar Maid. https://tinyurl.com/y3kc46a2
Page 5: Public Domain. Edward Burne-Jones. Study for the Soul Attains Pygmalion and Galatea. https://tinyurl.com/y5h6p9ut
Page 6: Public Domain. Harry D. William. https://tinyurl.com/yyf3usnl
Page 8: Public Domain. Bain News Service. https://tinyurl.com/yxzqdljo
Page 9: Public Domain. Esther Bubley. https://tinyurl.com/y3jynnum
Page 10: Public Domain. Albert Sands Southworth. Cropped. https://tinyurl.com/yxd6dfbv
Page 12: Public Domain. Anonymous.. Cropped. https://tinyurl.com/yxf6nrb7
Page 14: Public Domain. Anonymous. https://tinyurl.com/y2wkbk22

Page 15: Public Domain. Carl Mydans. https://tinyurl.com/y3o4eu77

Page 17: Public Domain. SS. https://tinyurl.com/y3e8svs9

Page 18: Public Domain. Cropped. *Galerie contemporaine, littéraire et artistique* . https://tinyurl.com/y2r8s8hv

Page 20: Public Domain. Unknown. Cropped. https://tinyurl.com/y4dfmulg

Page 21: Public Domain. SS. http://tinyurl.com/y5ksvyt7

Page 22: Public Domain. LHJ. http://tinyurl.com/yyuj2kop

Page 23: Public Domain. J. C Knowles Collection. Detail. http://tinyurl.com/y6rbfgb3

Page 25: Public Domain. SS. http://tinyurl.com/y6azz99j

Page 26: CC BY 3.0 (license link above). Vincente Martin from Fototeka Kutxa. http://tinyurl.com/y3mlagsl

Page 27: CC0 1.0 (license link above). Thomas Eakins. http://tinyurl.com/y294ct8p

Page 29: Public Domain. State Archivs of North Carolina. Cropped. https://tinyurl.com/y2mlzagw

Page 30-31: CC0 1.0 (license link above). Unknown. https://tinyurl.com/y4wfong7

Page 32: CC BY-SA 2.0 (license link above). Skagens Kunstmuseer. https://commons.wikimedia.org/wiki/File:HA_AA_HAF_8361_re_(37148493342).jpg

Page 33: CC0 1.0 (license link above). Gertrude Käsebier. https://tinyurl.com/y5cbhaek

Page 34: see page 23

Page 36: Public Domain. Elfelt. Cropped. https://commons.wikimedia.org/wiki/File:Woman_portrait_(5669537476).jpg

Page 37: Public Domain. John Vachon. https://tinyurl.com/yyro6yq4

Page 38: Public Domain. Paramount Pictures. Cropped. https://tinyurl.com/y3g3oqhx

Page 40: Public Domain. Unknown. https://commons.wikimedia.org/wiki/File:The_American_annual_of_photography_(1912)_(14785580543).jpg

Page 43: Public Domain. Australian War Memorial. Cropped. https://tinyurl.com/y2b7rnsn

Page 45: CC0 1.0 (license link above). Thomas Eakins. https://tinyurl.com/y52heh3v

Page 47: Public Domain, LHJ. https://commons.wikimedia.org/wiki/
File:The_Ladies%27_home_journal_(1948)_(14762448241).jpg
Page 49: Public Domain. Unknown. https://tinyurl.com/y4sqew4d
Page 51: Public Domain. African American Photographs Assembled for
1900 Paris Exposition. Cropped. https://tinyurl.com/y3gxg42g
Page 52: Public Domain. CC. https://tinyurl.com/yy57732w
Page 53: Public Domain. Jack Delano. https://tinyurl.com/yxu76rf4
Page 54: Public Domain. Russell Lee. Cropped.
https://www.loc.gov/pictures/item/2017735855/
Page 56: Public Domain. African American Photographs Assembled for
1900 Paris Exposition. Cropped. https://tinyurl.com/y2qmwpfv
Page 57: Public Domain. William Kinnimond Burton, a half-tone block
by I. Tanaka. https://tinyurl.com/yxc83lqj
Page 60: Public Domain. Davis & Company. Cropped.
https://tinyurl.com/y3o6w23j
Page 64: Public Domain. Thomas Eakins. https://tinyurl.com/y49sorl8
Page 65: Public Domain. Spaarnestad Photo Collection.
https://tinyurl.com/y37emr4c
Page 66: Public Domain. Egon Schiele. Madame Sohn.
https://tinyurl.com/y454kb94
Page 67: Public Domain. Jack Delano. https://tinyurl.com/yxfzzc8z
Page 68: Public Domain. [Maurice] Frink; restoration by Christoph
Braun. Cropped. https://tinyurl.com/yxj69968
Page 69: Public Domain, Library of Congress.
https://tinyurl.com/y2744vy8
Page 70: CC0 1.0 (license link above). Igor Ovsyannykov . Original is in
color. https://tinyurl.com/y3yp2aks
Page 73: Public Domain. Skitterphoto, Pixabay.com. https://tinyurl.com/
y6ardzrk
Page 74: Public Domain. Jack Delano. https://tinyurl.com/y582nvnt
Page 75: CC0 1.0 (license link above). Unplusunu.
https://tinyurl.com/y6rqdcmf
Page 76: Public Domain. Realart Pictures Corporation / Famous Players-
Lasky Corporation. Cropped. https://tinyurl.com/y6p3amz5
Page 77: CC0 1.0 (license link above). www.Pixel.la Free Stock Photos.
Original is in color. https://tinyurl.com/yybxmtga
Page 78: Public Domain. Jack Delano. https://tinyurl.com/yygmv9bv

Page 79: Public Domain. Julia Margaret Cameron. Cropped.
https://tinyurl.com/y59w6qnk

Page 80: Public Domain. Egon Schiele. Reclining Girl With Hair Mesh.
https://tinyurl.com/yydehryg

Page 81: Public Domain. Mary H. Mullen. https://tinyurl.com/y6ju2x8o

Page 82: Public Domain. Consuelo Kanaga.
https://tinyurl.com/y6cmpg62

Page 83: Public Domain. Dante Gabriel Rossetti. A Sea-Spell.
https://tinyurl.com/y458pbnd

Page 86: Public Domain. Frances Benjamin Johnston.
http://www.loc.gov/pictures/item/2001704030/

Page 87: Public Domain. Egon Schiele. Study To A Loving Nude.
https://tinyurl.com/y6dqv5cs

Page 88: Public Domain. Egon Schiele. Standing Girl.
https://tinyurl.com/y5qq7phf

Page 90: Public Domain. Sarah Maple. https://tinyurl.com/y4k9rgfu

Page 91: Public Domain. Egon Schiele. Two Women Embracing. https://
tinyurl.com/y3wzu6xw

Page 93: Public Domain. Egon Schiele. Edith Schiele With Her Nephew.
https://tinyurl.com/y69gfrd3

Page 94: Public Domain. James Jowers. https://tinyurl.com/y6ke987p

Page 96: Public Domain. Unknown. https://tinyurl.com/y3zyxo29

Page 98: Public Domain. PHCM Terry Mitchell.
https://tinyurl.com/yyw7xgxy

Page 99: Public Domain. Anne Brigman. https://tinyurl.com/y4rxh7hh

Page 101: Public Domain. Tyne & Wear Archives and Museums. https://
tinyurl.com/yxub8dsv
Public Domain. Tyne & Wear Archives and Museums.
https://tinyurl.com/y43rvpeh

Page 102: Public Domain. Jack Delano. https://tinyurl.com/y5mroxgr

Page 103: Public Domain. Egon Schiele. https://tinyurl.com/y29yz3ow

Page 105: Public Domain. Egon Schiele. https://tinyurl.com/y29yz3ow

Page 107: Public Domain. Frances Benjamin Johnston.
https://tinyurl.com/yxn56uru

Page 109: CC0 1.0 (license link above). Peter Oswald. Cropped. Original
is in color. https://tinyurl.com/y4gz9dch

Page 110: Public Domain. Gertrude Käsebier.

https://tinyurl.com/yxf932m6

Page 112: Public Domain. Eva Watson-Schütze .
https://tinyurl.com/y2kby75b

Page 114: Public Domain. Emily Mew. https://tinyurl.com/y3upk254

Page 116: Public Domain. Alice Boughton. https://tinyurl.com/yxscn56f

Page 118: Public Domain. James Jowers. https://tinyurl.com/yyqm6vw3

Page 120: Public Domain. Egon Schiele. Row of Trees.
https://tinyurl.com/y544x57x

Page 122: Public Domain. Egon Schiele. House and shed.
https://tinyurl.com/y3ylfb42

Page 123: Public Domain. Egon Schiele. Composition with three male
nudes. https://tinyurl.com/y4dzonpe

Page 125: Public Domain. Matson Collection.
https://tinyurl.com/y6t2ta94

Page 126: Public Domain. Anne W. Brigman.
https://tinyurl.com/yyqb7255

Page **129**: Public Domain. Ben Stahl. https://tinyurl.com/y3do9hym

Page **131**: CC0 1.0 (license link above). Frank Eugene.
https://tinyurl.com/y6f8myu7

Page **132**: Public Domain. Unknown. https://tinyurl.com/yxs38wwz

Page **134**: Public Domain. Stephanie Ludwig.
https://tinyurl.com/y6lq2jfw

Page **136**: Public Domain. Zaida Ben-Yusuf.
https://tinyurl.com/y25pk28r

Page **138**: Public Domain. Edith Emerson. https://tinyurl.com/yybn78jk

Page **139**: Public Domain. Dorsey. LHJ. https://tinyurl.com/y2dydo9r

Page **140**: CC0 1.0 (license link above). Egon Schiele. Portrait of Herbert
Rainer. https://tinyurl.com/y3dvbnzm

Page **141**: CC BY-SA 3.0 DE (license link above). Dorneth.
https://tinyurl.com/y39yhv9j

Page **143**: CC BY-SA 3.0 DE (license link above). Unknown.
https://tinyurl.com/y3vzftvq

Page **144**: Public Domain. Albert Reich. Cropped.
https://tinyurl.com/y5jb6w2e

Page **147**: Détourned version of poster on page 96

Page **149**: Public Domain. Unknown. Cropped.
https://tinyurl.com/yxdoqrn8

Page **151**: CCO 1.0 (license link above). Open Clip Art Library. https://tinyurl.com/yyeftgth

Page **153**: Public Domain. Frances Benjamin Johnston. https://tinyurl.com/y269ez26

Page **154**: CC BY 2.0 (license link above). Bartosz Brzeinski. Original is in color. https://tinyurl.com/y64o2zr8

Page **155**: Public Domain. Unknown. https://tinyurl.com/y54fqf3l

Page **157**: Public Domain. Étienne Carjat. https://tinyurl.com/yyheqexh

Page **160**: Public Domain. r Deng Nanguang. https://tinyurl.com/y3tr2v9k

Page **162**: Public Domain. LHJ. https://tinyurl.com/y6dv97j4

Page **163**: Public Domain. LHJ. https://tinyurl.com/yxg2lg6s

Page **165**: CCO 1.0 (license link above). Unknown. Cropped. Original is in color. https://tinyurl.com/y4onl2ey

Page **167**: Public Domain. Cândido Aragonez de Faria (Laranjeiras (Brésil), 12 août 1849 – Paris, 17 décembre 911). https://tinyurl.com/yy5v6dmb

Page **168**: Public Domain. Deseronto Archives. https://tinyurl.com/y45ptso6

Page **171**: Public Domain. George Eastman House. https://tinyurl.com/y6tv49dt

Page **172**: Public Domain. William Adolphe Bouguereau. Virgin and Lamb. https://tinyurl.com/y5p4p5st

Page **174**: Public Domain. Original Graphic by Rosina Plumley. Public Domain image is: Unknown. https://tinyurl.com/y3zao9fa

Page **175**: Public Domain. Pierre-Louise Pierson. https://tinyurl.com/y6fxompt

Page **176**: Public Domain. Original graphic by Rosina Plumley. Altered image is: Marion S. Trikosko. https://tinyurl.com/yyq4v5tp

Page **178**: Public Domain. Daily Mirror Photographer. https://tinyurl.com/y3r8hfjx

Page **180**: Public Domain. SS. https://tinyurl.com/y2c6ngo6

Page **183**: Public Domain. Consuelo Kanaga. https://tinyurl.com/y2butlxs

Page **185**: Public Domain. Original graphic by Rosina Plumley. Altered image is: Public Domain. Ernest L. Cranball. https://tinyurl.com/yy6l6no8

Page **186**: Public Domain. Egon Schiele. https://tinyurl.com/y29yz3ow

Page **187**: Public Domain. Carnby. https://tinyurl.com/y4oa4q5g

Page **189**: Public Domain. Original graphic by Rosina Plumley. Altered image is: Public Domain: Edward (Bliss) Foote. https://tinyurl.com/y4g8a6cy.

Page **190**: Public Domain. William Ridgway. Chatterton's Holiday Afternoon. https://tinyurl.com/y4nhm36e

Page **191**: Public Domain. Unknown. https://tinyurl.com/y5mln2jt

Page **193**: Public Domain. Thomas Rowlandson. Pigs at a Trough. https://tinyurl.com/y3jwk564

Page **194**: CCO 1.0 (license link above). Bulkan Evcimen. https://tinyurl.com/yxnkbesp

Page **197**: CCO 1.0 (license link above). Doris Ulmann. https://tinyurl.com/y38ja5xc

Pages **198 - 199**: Original graphic by Rosina Plumley.

Page **201**: Public Domain. Consuelo Kanaga. https://tinyurl.com/yxwn4e97

Page **203**: Public Domain. Famous Players. https://tinyurl.com/yxg9q35u

Page **204**: Public Domain. Caroline H. Gurrey. https://tinyurl.com/y3yqdddk

Page **206**: Public Domain. Caroline H. Gurrey. https://tinyurl.com/y2b2me5y

Page **208**: Public Domain. State Archives of North Carolina. https://tinyurl.com/y69bl2dr

Page **210**: Public Domain. Gertrude Käsebier. Cropped. https://tinyurl.com/y5v4926x

Page **211**: Public Domain. Alice Boughton. https://tinyurl.com/y553gp8r

Page **212**: Public Domain. Unknown. https://tinyurl.com/y3u6of74

Page **213**: Public Domain. Amelia Van Buren. https://tinyurl.com/y5l8vakq

Page **215**: Public Domain. Emma Goldman Papers UC Berkeley. https://tinyurl.com/y6rtehws

Page **215**: Donal McGraith.

Page **219**: Public Domain. See page 23.

Page **221**: CCO 1.0 (license link above). Nicolas Ladino Silva. https://tinyurl.com/y2g6n84u

Page **222**: Public Domain. Belizian. https://tinyurl.com/y37n6y98

Page **225**:

Public Domain. African American Photographs Assembled for 1900 Paris Exposition. Cropped. https://tinyurl.com/y45dnt96

Public Domain. Caroline H. Gurrey. Cropped. https://tinyurl.com/yxvxkbvs

Public Domain. Robert Demachy. https://tinyurl.com/y4rc6orl

Public Domain. William Crooke. Cropped. https://tinyurl.com/y4scqh8q

Page **226**:

Public Domain. Thomas Eakins. Cropped. https://tinyurl.com/y3a9lomx

Public Domain. Marion Post Wolcott. Cropped. https://tinyurl.com/yxtjl8wc

Public Domain. African American Photographs Assembled for 1900 Paris Exposition. Cropped. https://tinyurl.com/y5b48n33

Public Domain. Rondal Partridge. Cropped. https://tinyurl.com/y37lbd9p

Page **227**: CC BY-SA 2.0 (license link above). Skagens Kunstmuseer. Cropped. https://tinyurl.com/y4kedpve

Page **228**: Public Domain. Jack Delano. Cropped. https://tinyurl.com/y6k39c7x

Page **231**: Public Domain. Mississippi Department of Archives and History. https://tinyurl.com/y36j4kt8

Page **233**: CC BY 2.0 (license link above). Becker1999, from Grove City OH. https://tinyurl.com/y3vg6lzq

Page **234**: Public Domain. Mary Carnell. https://tinyurl.com/y4emqtec

Page **236**: Public Domain. Beverly Bennett Dobbs. https://tinyurl.com/y35glsb5

Page **237**: Public Domain. Egon Schiele. Lovers (Self-portrait with Wally). https://tinyurl.com/y3pqlkec

Inconsequential Diversions

For information on Inconsequential Diversions visit:
https://inconsequentialdiversions.wordpress.com/

About the *raindrips to Rethfernhim Series*:

The novels in this series combine genre fiction with art, commentary, and photography. Meant to be art objects, they are ontological mysteries which focus on the death of reality.

Also in the *raindrips to Rethfernhim Series*:

The Lingering Longing for a Long Lost Love
by Rosina Plumley and Rod Dubey

*an ontological mystery with
photographs and other lies*

An experimental mystery novel consisting of 60 found photographs, each followed by one or two pages of text. It purports to be the journal of Gerald Conway recounting his investigation into the 1946 bombing of a train station. The target and motive are a mystery. Was it attempted murder, sabotage, or simply spectacle?

Rod Dubey provides editorial commentary on subjects suggested by the story, ranging from post-war America to the dubiousness of the narrative, ontological crisis, noir films about trains, the post-war proliferation of images and simulation, and the significance of trains to war, capitalism, and planetary destruction.

www.ingramcontent.com/pod-product-compliance
Lightning Source LLC
Chambersburg PA
CBHW071144180726
48291CB00007B/2325